The Hotel Mandolin

A New Orleans Paranormal Mystery

by
Evelyn Klebert

The Hotel Mandolin
A New Orleans Paranormal Mystery
By Evelyn Klebert

A Cornerstone Book
Published by Cornerstone Book Publishers
An Imprint of Michael Poll Publishing

First Cornerstone edition 2014
Second Cornerstone edition 2019
Third Cornerstone edition 2023

Cornerstone Book Publishers
Hot Springs Village, AR
www.cornerstonepublishers.com

ISBN: 978-1-61342-290-8

Dedication

For Robert and Jonathan,
whose insatiable thirst for knowledge never ceases to be
an inspiration.

Table of Contents

The Hotel Mandolin

A New Orleans Paranormal Mystery

Cassie Breslin

One

Cassie Breslin felt a restlessness stirring in her bones. She wasn't a young woman anymore, forty-eight, two years from fifty, and she wasn't an old woman. Although, in some ways, it felt that way, as though life should have settled now into its familiar pattern, a paradigm for what the rest of her years might look like. That's what her mind told her. But her skin, her bones, her blood, and yes, of course, her heart, which spoke to her more clearly than any tangible thought, told her differently — told her that something was out there, something beyond the walls of this house.

She sank into one of the pale blue armchairs facing the fireplace, feeling slightly deflated. It was frustrating and intangible. She wondered, quite distinctly, if this feeling was simply concocted from a tired mind.

"So, you're sure you'll be all right while I'm gone?"

Smiling, she glanced across the den to Elise standing in the doorway. "Yes, of course," she answered with as much summed-up animation as she could muster.

She rose from the chair and crossed to her dark-haired sister, who had not moved. Elise was staring at her, or rather staring through her, with an expression that conveyed that she was not pleased with what she saw. "Why are you so unhappy, Cassie?" she asked softly.

She allowed the false smile to drop from her face to be replaced by the pensiveness she felt. "It's not unhappy,

Elise. It's restlessness. Maybe I need to find another job just to get out of the house."

"I wish you'd come with me."

"To Southern France?" she laughed. "I think I'd just hold you back right now."

"That's not why," Elise said flatly. "Something is keeping you here."

Cassie stared at her a bit blankly, not really understanding, but again feeling that intangible tug as though there was something, something to do. "Timing, I think."

Elise nodded slowly, "Yes, I can see that. Be careful, Cassandra. Be wary."

She laughed softly, "Shouldn't I be saying that to you? After all, I'll be home. What could happen to me here?"

"What did the police find?"

Peter Norfleet shook his head. "Nothing out of the ordinary, ruled it a suicide, overdose of anti-depressants she was taking."

Max Gravier unpredictably prowled the small hotel room. He would touch things briefly — the curtains, the espresso-colored dresser, even the walls — caught up in some deep exploration that Peter didn't really understand. But he had spent some years in acquaintance with the man, noting that this was how he gleaned his information. "But the parents— "

"The parents aren't satisfied. They claim she had plans to attend graduate school at Tulane, had a scholarship, too much to look forward to."

Again, Max began to canvas the room slowly. Peter knew it was a long shot bringing in Max at this point. The room had been cleaned, even occupied by a few guests since the suicide. The Hotel Mandolin was a prestigious establishment in New Orleans and had been so since the turn of the century. So, it was easy enough for them to hush up that there had recently been a suicide in one of their rooms. "It's difficult," Max whispered, almost to himself.

"Anything you pick up," Peter muttered, sinking onto the queen-sized bed. It wasn't the nicest room in the hotel, just a middle-of-the-road one. Years ago, he'd stayed in a suite with his ex-wife, quite luxurious, quite impressive. He held back a deep sigh somewhere in the vicinity of his chest. He hated these cases, so much emotion and upset from the parents — just wanting some sort of thread, anything to cling to that might make sense out of senselessness. Unfortunately, all his years on the police force had taught him quite succinctly that, too often, the world left us hanging with that feeling of desolation and no magic answer to ease the despair.

Max paused, staring out the window and shaking his head. "There's some impediment here."

"Here specifically?" Peter asked.

"Hard to say, something with the hotel, I think. Does it have a history?"

"A history?"

"A history of paranormal activity?" Max said pointedly.

The business offices of The Hotel Mandolin were located beneath the main lobby of the establishment. Peter and Max took an elevator down for two purposes: to return the key to room 503, the hotel room where Janie Tyler had taken her own life; and to quiz Peter's connection here — John McGinty. McGinty was one of the assistant managers and evidently someone who owed his friend Peter Norfleet a favor. Clearly, it was dangerous to owe a private investigator a favor because, sooner or later, it would be collected on.

Max closed his eyes, trying to clear his mind as they descended from the fifth floor. His head was aching. It was odd that he had spent his whole life in New Orleans but had never crossed the threshold of this historic and quite posh New Orleans establishment. It was located on Carondelet St., right in the heart of the business district. It had been reputed to have housed presidents, governors, and a whole array of politicians over the years. However, he had perhaps unconsciously avoided it for some reason, and now it was becoming clear why. His head continued to throb from the barrage of heavy energies that seemed to swirl about the place. As the old saying goes, *"Everything that glitters isn't gold—"*

"All right?" Peter asked him.

His eyes flickered open. "Yes, your hotel is giving me a headache."

He nodded, "Yeah, I'm not too fond of it as well, although I couldn't tell you exactly why."

Max smiled. His friend Peter Norfleet was a mass of contradictions. He thought, at times, that was why they'd hit it off so well. He was well into middle age and an avid history buff, particularly of the city. He appeared sedate, laid back, but had rough edges that could slice like a knife if you got too close. He had a razor-sharp memory of facts, almost photographic, and was quite possibly the best at his job he'd ever seen but didn't seem to particularly enjoy it. And beyond all of this, he had instincts, instincts that Max suspected were psychic in nature, but that was a thought that Peter Norfleet refused to entertain. In his mind, he was still a cop and would always be just a cop who didn't have his badge anymore.

"So, your friend John McGinty, would you call him trustworthy?"

"No, not especially."

Nervous, that was how Max sized up John McGinty, trying to retain his veneer of smoothness but deep down exceedingly jumpy. "I don't know if I really understand your question." He responded from behind his moderately sized, mahogany-finished desk. McGinty was only one of the assistant managers of the hotel. And his office reflected just that, not too big — in truth, a bit on the smallish side, the desk itself taking up a large balance of the room. He seemed to be somewhere around Max's age, early thirties, well-groomed, oily black, short hair in a navy-blue suit.

Peter glanced at Max to repose the question that he'd offered concerning paranormal activity in the hotel. "Ghosts, psychic activity, moving objects, sightings, weird occurrences."

McGinty's eyes widened, "Of course, we have weird occurrences, but that's just the overflow from the French Quarter crowd."

"So that's a NO?" Max asked, feeling less than diplomatic. He couldn't help it. This place was getting to him.

"Well, gentleman, there will always be stories about places as old as this one. You know, The Hotel Mandolin goes back to the 1880s, and there have been deaths here, mobsters in the twenties. But you know people's imaginations. Can we close the book on this suicide, sad affair, but nothing really to it, don't you think?"

Max glanced at Peter, who was eying him without expression. Sometimes he really played it way too close to the vest. "I'd like to try one more thing. I have a friend who might be able to help."

Peter said, "Yes, John, we'll need to see the room again. How about holding out on more guests there for a little while longer?"

McGinty grimaced. Max could read him loud and clear. He wanted this business over with. "I can give you the week, gentleman. That's all. Keep the key but get it back to me on Friday."

Peter nodded, "Good enough." And then he left the room abruptly, leaving Max to do nothing but follow him.

"Barbequing? It's November."

"Your Aunt likes to barbeque, and she'll be gone for three weeks."

"It's cold."

"Bundle up, Jared. Besides, you can do it early."

"It's already three."

Cassie sighed with exaggerated exasperation. It was getting difficult to get anyone to do anything for her these days. Even though she'd moved back home, her daughter Caroline was gone nearly all the time, and Jared, her youngest, was following the same path. She wondered dismally why she was keeping this big house at all. Luckily, her late husband had left enough savings and investments to care for her financially. But she was beginning to feel like a ghost bashing around in this place, all alone most of the time. "Fine, I'll do it myself."

Jared frowned at her with that particularly unique way her nineteen-year-old son had mastered. "No Mom, I will put on my coat and barbeque out in the cold to please Aunt Elise." Then he turned, heading out of the kitchen to the back porch, where she could hear the screen door slam loudly behind him. Off to prep the pit, she surmised. Lovely, what she needed to make today perfect was attitude.

"Mom," Caroline seemed to come out of nowhere. Cassie hadn't even realized she was in the house.

"Oh, hi dear, dinner will be around five. Jared is barbequing. Is Max coming?"

Her daughter smiled a bit broadly, which put Cassie on alert. She always knew when she was being handled, particularly by her children. "Yes, and he's bringing a friend."

Cassie's hands froze over the sink where she'd been cleaning lettuce for a salad. "What did you say?" she said softly.

"He asked if he could bring someone, a friend of his. I told him it would be fine."

"Caroline! This is supposed to be a family dinner for your Aunt."

"I know. It just seemed important. Something is going on. I could tell by his voice. Max wouldn't have asked unless there was some reason."

Cassie sighed deeply. She wasn't in the mood to play the hostess for strangers. She was too much out of sorts. "All right, all right, you set the table, Caroline, and add a plate."

"Thanks, Mom."

"Does Max's friend have a name?"

"Peter Norfleet."

She nodded begrudgingly, "Fine, I hope he likes barbeque."

Peter Norfleet

Two

Peter followed Max in his brown sedan feeling a bit wary. Crashing family celebrations was not his style. Even attending family celebrations felt more than uncomfortable these days. Of course, that was the fringe benefit of being divorced. Even being so for ten years did not completely erase the awkwardness. His ex-wife was remarried with two children from her new relationship. Fortunately, the new husband was cordial with the old Dad, and he was always invited to significant events, birthdays, graduation parties. Everyone was friendly, though he couldn't shake the feeling that he was just the fifth wheel. He was the spare tire that had a flat and wasn't even carried in the car anymore, just discarded. But it wasn't as though he expected any different or was particularly depressed about it. Peter Norfleet was a realistic man, not filled with expectations, just one who took life as it came.

"Maybe we shouldn't just drop in on them like this."

"No, I was invited."

"But I wasn't."

And then Max had smiled with an odd gleam in his eyes. "It's okay. You are now."

He wondered vaguely if he were dressed appropriately. He wore a dark olive-colored sports jacket over khakis and a dark brown fedora his daughter Jessie had given him last Christmas. It was his normal fare when he was on a case, but now he was headed to a different event, a social event, changing modes. Peter had hit fifty last year, a time when one would think a man should be settled in his skin. However, as it was, the only thing that seemed certain was that everything was always changing.

"Now, I am asking for your discretion. This family is an unusual one, very gifted but also highly private. They wouldn't want anything to get out about them publicly."

"Sort of like you."

Max nodded with a smile. "Yes, but let's just say I'm very protective of them."

"Any one of them in particular?"

Max never called her his girlfriend. But several months earlier, Peter had become aware that Max Gravier was seeing someone, seeing someone quite frequently. Peter had called to invite him over for a ball game or to have a late dinner in the quarter. Lately, the answer was always *No*. He was seeing Caroline tonight. Girlfriend? No, good friend. Perhaps that designation had some significance in the realm of psychics that he was unaware of. Still, he'd never mentioned that she had special "gifts" until today in the lobby of The Hotel Mandolin.

"She might be able to help with Janie Tyler." And then, it became that perhaps some other member of her family might aid them as well.

Peter had become intrigued and, yes, desperate, having hit one brick wall after another with this case. So naturally, now he was attending a family dinner.

Max pulled his SUV into a long arching driveway on the side of a Victorian-style home on the corner of Prytania Street. This was New Orleans's Garden District, quite a neighborhood and quite a lovely house. As Peter stepped out of his car, which he'd parked just behind Max's, he took a deep breath and tried to shake off his crusty investigator demeanor to become a bit more affable. That was if he could even remember how that went.

Caroline Breslin, a lovely young brunette in her mid-twenties, walked out the front door heading toward Max. He was speaking to another man just in front of his car. She knew Max had a mysterious meeting with his friend Peter Norfleet, his current companion, a few days ago. But something was notably different in his call to her about bringing Peter with him to dinner. It was a bit out of character for Max, although in truth, she'd only known him for just over three months. At times though, it really seemed much longer, and at others, as though they'd met just yesterday.

Max smiled at her approach. His eyes searched hers for an explanation. It wasn't like her to come outside to meet him, but there was a palpable anxiety floating about the house that she needed to escape.

"Caroline," he murmured, giving her a quick hug. "This is my friend Peter Norfleet."

She reached out and, grasping his hand felt an odd surge of familiarity, not unlike something she'd forgotten. "Good to meet you, Mr. Norfleet."

"Please, Peter."

She smiled nodding, "Everything all right?" Max asked, clearly picking up on her nervousness.

"Yeah, I mean, Mom seems a bit rattled. I think it's Aunt Elise's going out of the country." She shrugged, "I don't think she trusts airplanes."

Peter responded amiably, "Well, I'm sure she's not alone in that opinion."

Caroline continued to try to place the peculiar reaction she'd had to him. At the very least, he was good-looking, which might put her Mom in a better mood. Then again, maybe not. Hard to tell with Cassie Breslin.

"So, who is this fellow Max is bringing to dinner?"

11

Cassie's nerves were stretching tautly now. For some reason, she regretted everything now, the dinner, the invitation. She would have preferred to let the day go by quietly. "He's a friend of Max. Caroline says he's a PI."

"A private investigator! Do you really want a private investigator in your house, Cassie?"

She spun around, feeling intently for the moment that she might want to throw Elise's barbeque in her face. "Well, since I fenced the crown jewels, I feel pretty confident that he won't slap on the handcuffs."

"He's a PI Mom, not a cop. He doesn't arrest people," Jared snickered a bit at her expense.

"Mom, Max, and Peter are here," Caroline called from the den.

"Oh good, hide the contraband," Cassie whispered hotly.

Elise grimaced for a moment. "Cassie, you need to calm down. How about a glass of wine?"

Behind her, Jared patted her shoulder. "Yeah, take it easy, Mom. I'm the one barbequing in the freezing cold."

Cassie leaned back in a chair at her dining room table and sipped a glass of white Riesling wine. It was a long rectangular, pine wood table she bought at an arts and crafts fair in Lafitte parish just three years earlier. Originally, this spacious room just off the kitchen had housed a rather formal table, black oak, that Allen had picked out for entertaining his business acquaintances. He had been a regional manager at an oil company in the city. He had started as an engineer but had quickly worked himself up the cooperate ladder. Naturally, entertaining had become a key in that particular equation, although Cassie didn't like it. She became accomplished at it but always felt a bit of an aversion to the people who routinely were milling about her house. Although, in those days, she'd considered it more Allen's home, as was the dining table. So, replacing it was an easy call, particularly when she spotted this one — simple, rustic, and not in the least formal. She'd even contracted the carpenter to create chairs for her, all made of pine.

She sat at the end of the table, feeling more relaxed. The barbeque had been informal, everyone pitching in, even Mr. Norfleet or Peter, as he'd insisted everyone call him. He was, well, the only way Cassie could describe him, mysterious or, perhaps better said, unexpected. He was a fairly tall man, though not quite as tall as Caroline's Max, dark-haired, ever so slightly unshaven though not to the degree that he was unkempt. And with rather light blue-grayish eyes that seemed filled with humor at one moment but strangely intense and watchful the next. She'd asked herself if she thought him handsome. Caroline quickly mentioned that he was just a bit older than Cassie. Handsome? She didn't know. She'd stopped thinking about men that way for some time. But interesting? Intriguing? Most certainly.

So, all was going well, and despite her anxiety and Jared's histrionics about the barbequing, he'd done a wonderful job — ribs, burgers, chicken, and even hot dogs. It was plenty of food that would last for days to come, although most of the time it seemed just her alone.

"Well, this was a wonderful meal. Thank you to Jared, the cook, and Cassie for making us all feel welcome," Max declared.

Cassie smiled. Caroline looked at him, delighted. She could tell those two were growing closer, and she felt comforted in that. He was a good man.

"Yes, thank you all for the lovely send-off for my trip," Elisa echoed graciously.

"We'll miss you," Cassie murmured to her sister.

Cassie's eyes flickered again over to Max, and she stopped. The anxiety she'd felt earlier suddenly surged up again. "There is something I wanted to mention," he began.

She waited, saying nothing, just watching him. Then her eyes passed over Peter Norfleet beside him. He looked uncomfortable. "As you know, Peter here is a Private Investigator, and I have on occasion consulted on some of his cases."

Cassie took a sip of wine. It was an odd feeling that she was experiencing. Although her mind told her succinctly this was the beginning of something, it felt very much like the aftermath.

"Are you working on a case now Peter?" Caroline asked.

"Yes, as a matter of fact, Max and I had just returned from the Hotel Mandolin."

There seemed to be an indefinable pause for a moment. "What did you say?" Elise asked with an edge in her voice.

"I'm investigating a suicide at the Hotel Mandolin."

"Yes," Max continued slowly, "I was hoping to ask for Caroline's help, but given the events of several months ago, I thought perhaps we could all discuss it."

Cassie's head had begun to reel. The mention of that place brought a feeling of iciness to her blood. Slowly, she placed the wine glass on the table. "I'm afraid that's impossible, Max. I'm sorry Mr. Norfleet. We can't help you."

Caroline's eyes widened at the suddenness of her emphatic pronouncement. "Don't you think that's rather my decision, Mom?"

"Caroline, that hotel is a very difficult place," Elise insisted.

"Yes, I'm sure, but if I could help."

Then in a move that completely startled Cassie, Peter Norfleet stood up. "I'm sorry. I certainly don't want to cause problems in your family. We'll find another way," he stated. "If you'll excuse me, I don't want to intrude any further."

As he quickly strode out of the room, Cassie felt profoundly like she'd been punched. And she did something that she had no explanation for. She rose to her feet and followed him.

He was hurriedly moving toward the front door when Cassie Breslin called from behind. "Please, Mr. Norfleet, I didn't mean you should leave."

He stopped with surprise and turned around slowly. Cassie stood in front of him, eyes filled with distress. She was really quite lovely – blonde, hair pulled up in a soft bun, and those blue eyes. "I'm sorry," he said. "I think Max shouldn't have brought this up at all. I ruined your lovely dinner."

She looked at him intently, trying to make sense of him somehow. "No, it's just." She sighed a bit, "Has Max told you about us?"

"Sketchily, you're all gifted. You're all private. He's crazy about your daughter."

"Yes, I guess all of that's true. Caroline has been through a difficult time lately. I suppose I'm protective."

"As you should be," he said softly.

"And that hotel."

"Yes, you mentioned that."

"It's a difficult place. I went there once with my late husband. I don't think I slept a wink."

He looked at her oddly, "That bad? I'm afraid I'm a bit thicker-skinned than Max. I didn't pick up too much on my visits there."

"Well," she smiled at him in a way that drew him in easily. "Be happy that you didn't. Your case, Max said it was a suicide."

"Yes, just a bit younger than your Caroline. Her parents are devastated. Just need to understand why, and honestly, I have nothing to give them."

Those eyes, those lovely blue eyes, seemed to overflow with compassion. "Peter, will you come back in

15

so all of us can talk this over? Maybe there is some way we can try to help you."

"Cassie, I really don't want to intrude."

"No, it feels like something we need to do."

The Hotel Mandolin

Three

Cassie had managed to retrieve Peter Norfleet
from his rather abrupt exit. Why exactly he was leaving
so quickly, she had no idea, and why she felt so
compelled to stop him was even a greater mystery to
her. It was an impulse born of some empathic pull that
caused her to chase him down. She hoped dearly that it
wasn't at its core something as inane as needing to be
the perfect hostess left over from her years with Allen.

Whatever the case, once he'd explained the
suffering of poor Janie Tyler's parents, she knew things
had shifted. She didn't give herself credit for having the
sensitivities of her daughter Caroline, but when it came
to mothers particularly and their children. Well, there
was the Achilles' heel. Once Peter Norfleet returned to
the dining room, she compelled her children, and as it
was everyone else, to clear the table for coffee and
dessert. Luckily, Elise's favorite wasn't ice cream but
instead strawberry shortcake.

As Caroline passed out plates of the frothy
concoction, Cassie settled back in her chair, trying to
figure out how to make this work. "So, I thought we
could discuss this a bit as a family." She stated more
calmly than she felt. Of course, she knew everyone's
eyes were on her, particularly Max and Peter's, who
clearly weren't family.

"I thought you were dead set against this," Elise
murmured loudly enough for everyone to hear.

"Yes, well, I realized that maybe I had been rash. Maybe that was a knee-jerk reaction. I want to know what you all think about it."

"What exactly did you have in mind?" Elise asked, directing her question to Peter.

"Well, I just hoped Caroline and whoever else might want to come along would take a look at the room where the girl died, see if they pick up any impressions," his voice sort of drifted off with the vagueness of what he was asking.

"You said she killed herself, this girl," Jared piped in.

"Yes, it seemed to be an overdose of anti-depressants," Peter stated rather flatly.

"Mr. Norfleet said her parents are very upset. They can't understand why she would do such a thing." He flashed a look at her at the use of the name Mr. Norfleet. Oh yes, he wanted to be called Peter, but strangely it felt a bit awkward to her.

"I don't like that place," Elise muttered. "And I won't be here to help you all. What do you think, Caroline?" she asked directly.

Caroline seemed stoic for a moment, as though considering. "Well, Max will be there. I don't see the harm in trying. I would like to think that I could be of some help to people."

Cassie eyed her daughter quietly. It was true when Max came into their lives. It had ignited something in Caroline, a desire to truly use her gifts. She would be a poor mother indeed if she tried to stand in her way.

"Cassie, maybe if you went too."

She glanced with a bit of surprise at Elise. "Well, I don't know if I'd be of any help. I don't have Caroline's gifts."

"You're wrong, Cassie. You're very perceptive."

"Yes, I think you're right." She looked up in surprise into the very focused eyes of Peter Norfleet, just a few people down the table from her. "If you would consider it, Mrs. Breslin, I think it would be an excellent idea."

Caroline echoed, "I think so too. Feels right."

She put her small coffee mug to her lips to give her time to digest the turn of events, the least of which was Peter Norfleet's use of the name Mrs. Breslin. Evidently, he was trying to make a point. But given everything, she had no idea how she truly felt about it. "Well, when could you arrange for us to see the room?" she asked calmly.

"How about tomorrow night?"

"Dang it, I can't make it," Jared muttered. "Night class."

Cassie again briefly met the eyes of Peter Norfleet, who was sipping his coffee. He was up to something, but what in the world could it be?

"That is an interesting man," Elise murmured over a sink of dirty dishes.

"You know, I can finish this. You should get home and rest. You have to be up early for your flight."

Her younger sister laughed behind her. "Are you just going to ignore my comment?"

"What? The *'That is an interesting man'* one?"

"Yes, filled with so many complexities, quite compelling."

"Well, then maybe Max can set you up with him."

Her dark green eyes met Cassie's shrewdly. "Well, that would be a waste. I'm psychic enough to know he's already intrigued with my sister."

"I'm sure that's not true," Cassie murmured.

"You know, you really need to stop this down-on-yourself attitude. You're a lovely, vibrant woman."

"Nearly fifty."

"As is he, from what I understand."

"Look, I've had a complex man in my life. It didn't turn out so well."

"Allen wasn't all that complex. That was the problem. Anyway, it doesn't matter if you want to hide from life, Cassandra. It has a way of finding you."

She sighed deeply, "Well, finish up the dishes. We have a busy day tomorrow." That was her way of ending the conversation. She wouldn't consider Peter Norfleet that way. The last thing she wanted was any complications of this sort.

"Well, what's on your mind?"

"What?" Caroline answered with distraction.

After seeing Peter off, Max had decided he needed some alone time with Caroline, so they'd headed out for a late-night drive. "Are you worried about going to the hotel? I can cancel it if you like."

"No, it's not that. At least, I don't think so. I'm thinking of moving out again."

"Ah, do you think it's been long enough?"

"I don't know. I'm feeling uneasy."

Max squeezed her hand, feeling some of her anxiety seep into him. "It seems to be a bit more than just that."

"I guess. I can't put my finger on it. It just feels as though something is coming."

He nodded, "Yes, I know exactly what you mean."

He drove around for a bit, trying to sift through the various impressions he'd received at dinner tonight. Max had intimated that the Breslin family was a gifted one. Without explanation, Peter had come to the impression that he meant one whose members were psychically inclined, as was Max.

But he hadn't expected the odd connectedness and rapport of the family. Caroline, the daughter who

Peter was more than sure his friend was falling in love with, seemed a bit on the vulnerable side to him while the Aunt was aggressively protective of them all. The son seemed like a young bright kid, not so unlike his own son Caleb, just a few years older. And then there was Cassie, Cassie Breslin. Now this, he hadn't expected – delicate, lovely on the surface but turbulent beneath the skin. It was almost unnerving being near her. So quickly did he seem to glean her thoughts. He had no idea exactly what had propelled him to leave the dinner table so abruptly, only that the impressions flooding over him were overwhelming. He needed some air to get to a place he recognized.

But then, she'd followed him. And he allowed himself to be pulled in, pulled into her empathy. It was heady stuff to be talked to so kindly and intimately by such a lovely woman. He had toughened himself in response to a harsh world for some time, but here, this stranger seemed to be so easily melting that defensive shield.

He tried to shake it off as he drove around the city in the darkness. He was a fool, and he had a crush. It was as simple as that, he told himself, though his instincts whispered to him succinctly that nothing about this would be simple.

"Now, don't forget when you go into that place, create a bubble of white light around you."

"Bubble?"

Elise frowned, "You know what I mean, to protect yourself."

"All right, but what exactly is causing the problem?"

"At the hotel? I don't know. I've always avoided it, just subconsciously avoided it. I can't investigate every haunted or problematic nook in New Orleans. It would take several lifetimes."

Well, that was true enough. "Yes, I suppose so." It had been a conversation earlier that morning, just outside the metal detectors at the airport.

"You were the one who spent a night there with Allen. What did you feel?"

So long ago to try to resurrect that memory, "Hard to say, the place was gorgeous, opulent. And they had that club in the lobby, The Cavern."

"Oh yes, is it still there?"

"No idea, you better go. Have fun."

"All right, and remember, keep your wits about you," and that was the last thing Elise had said before she was swallowed up by the long lines of the New Orleans Municipal Airport.

As promised, Jared disappeared about an hour before Max came to pick up Caroline and Cassie to bring them to the Hotel Mandolin. Peter Norfleet, or rather Peter, a designation she was finding difficult to refer to him as, for some obscure reason, would be meeting them. Apparently, he had an apartment in the warehouse district. It was the latest trend in the city to convert those old buildings into massive condominiums. She never imagined herself living in that sort of setup, but then again, things were changing — children moving on with their own lives. She wondered with distraction if she would indeed want to hang onto the Prytania Street house if she ended up there alone.

These were the thoughts that occupied her mind as they walked along Carondelet St. toward the Hotel Mandolin. It wasn't long, however, before she was drawn back into the present as they came closer. It was early November, and the chill of the night air swept around her, reminding her candidly of Elise's parting words. *"Keep your wits about you."*

The gleaming brass-accented entranceway seemed to loom over them in an oppressive way she didn't remember feeling nearly twenty years before. But then again, she was a different woman back then. She deliberately cloaked herself in a protective white light before she followed Max and Caroline across the threshold — the threshold into the great golden revolving doors that led into the hotel.

Voices

Four

Were they always unhappy?

The gleaming chandeliers with their exquisite tiers of crystals glittered across the expansive ceiling that seemed to stretch on indefinitely.

"Come on, Cassie, what do you think? Not bad."

He'd had his arm around her holding her close, and he was young. She remembered him young and vibrant, filled with unabashed enthusiasm.

"It's beautiful," she'd said, caught up in that little bubble of happiness that seemed spun so tightly around them. But back then, when her eyes canvassed the lush lobby of the Hotel Mandolin, they didn't stop. They didn't hesitate to take in details like the smooth but intricate design of its arching coffered ceiling overhead, the quiet dignity of its block-long row of golden columns, or the endless stretch of mosaic floor beckoning visitors inward. Back then, she hadn't noticed much of anything. Perhaps that was a special protection of youth. Would anyone really go forward if they truly saw what was there?

"Mom," Cassie pulled herself out of her distracted musings.

She glanced about, not realizing she'd stopped in the middle of the lobby. Everyone else stood near the elevator, its burnished golden doors gaping open, waiting none too patiently. "Sorry," she murmured, just catching Peter Norfleet's eyes as she stepped through its threshold.

"I don't know, Max. Maybe we shouldn't be dragging these people into this."

"You mean Caroline?"

"And Cassandra, I don't know, doesn't feel quite right."

"You want me to cancel?" Max responded flatly.

Was that really what he wanted? Peter wandered out through the sliding glass doors onto the balcony of his Julia St. condo. It was late the same evening as the get-together at Cassie Breslin's house, and it was gnawing on him that he was somehow opening a can of worms by bringing these people into this. He didn't have the right to insinuate himself into that lovely, serene woman's life. "Pete, you still there?"

"Yeah, just considering your question."

He detected some frustration from his usually inordinately patient friend on the other end of the line. "Well, look, we'll make it simple — a quick visit and then let it go, just a quick exploratory visit, no harm."

Peter considered grimly. How many times had he heard that through the years? No harm, just simple, and then the unseen gunpowder explodes. But then again, poor Clara and Josh Tyler were grieving for their daughter Janie. It pained him. Strange at what peculiar moments, he was reminded he still had a heart, which could bleed for others. "Right, sorry to call so late. This case, it's getting to me."

"There's a lot of upset here."

"Yes, the family's."

"That's some of it," Max replied without further explanation.

"I don't understand. There's nothing here. I mean, so many people have been here. There should be something, but not a trace, not a trace of her."

"How can that be? There must have been strong emotion to drive her to do such a thing."

She heard the voices but said nothing.

"Try again, just for a bit," she heard Max say.

"You know, there aren't always answers. Perhaps you shouldn't push too hard," Peter's voice. What she felt was such an odd sensation, as though she were hearing from a distant hollow place like an echo off a cold metal wall.

"Are you all right?" Peter Norfleet's hand on her arm sent a shock into her skin, yanking her back from that strange disconnected place. And he was there in front of her, staring at her with those eyes as though trying to see right inside her. "You look pale," he said. She glanced around the room. Max and Caroline were sitting on the queen-sized bed's edge, whispering, not even audible. But moments before, she could hear them quite clearly, although in that strange metallic-like tone.

"I'm fine," Cassie murmured, lying. And glancing again at his face, she clearly felt he knew it. But he stepped back, giving her a quick nod. "Are you picking up anything?" she directed with distraction to Caroline and Max.

"I don't know," Caroline said with exasperation. "It's strange, as though it's muffled here."

Max nodded, "That's what I sensed, some sort of block."

Caroline stood up, walking over to her. "Are you feeling anything, Mom?"

Cassie felt a bit surprised. Her gifts had never been of the same overt nature as her sister's and daughter's. "I don't know, just disoriented. Maybe if we could walk through more of the hotel, whatever is going on here seems a bit broader than this room."

Max looked at her with interest, then turned to Peter. "Do you mind? It's worth a shot."

He nodded, taking out his phone. "I'll try to get someone here to show us around."

Rick Lightner was a tall, energetic, sandy-haired bellboy that Cassie estimated couldn't have had more than a year or two on Jared. He'd arrived at the door of Room 503 with a broad smile and a curious attitude.

"So, Mr. McGinty has sent me up to show you around the Mandolin. I'll do my best, but I've only actually been working here a few months, between semesters at the University or rather taking a brief break," he rambled on. He was animated, smiling broadly at them the whole time he rattled off his discourse. "So, where would you all like to start?"

It was disconcerting that Rick Lightner had so effectively filled the silent room with noise. Cassie had failed to realize that it had been indeed silent and actually quite awkward. Caroline, leaning against Max and looking a bit pale, said in a very low voice, "Mom?"

Oh, right, this was her idea, and at the moment, it seemed she was leading the charge.

"The kitchens," she said flatly, having no idea where that idea had come from.

Max's eyes widened a bit, "Really?"

And then Peter was beside her, "Yes, is that a problem, Mr. Lightner?"

"Well, I suppose not," he muttered, "if I can remember how to get there."

"Can we take the stairs?" Cassie blurted out again. Why exactly, she wasn't sure, but it felt as though something was filtering in.

"The stairs?" Rick repeated. "That's the long way, but sure let's give it a try," he said light-heartedly. But all Cassie could feel were all the eyes on her questioning her rather unorthodox choices.

"What's going on?" Caroline whispered as they walked through one of the spacious kitchens tucked away on the hotel's ground floor.

They were all a bit out of breath, having descended five flights of stairs, but there had been something about the staircase — its dark golden carpet and heavy oak railing and balusters. Looking down the stairwell as they descended had sent her mind into a dizzying vertigo so much that Peter Norfleet had caught her arm several times to steady her.

And now, here they were in the midst of this tremendous cold, essentially white room, which also felt just eerie. Cassie could feel anxiety wrapping around her. The ceiling was impossibly high and even filled with its staff, the space engulfed them. Its ceramic floor echoed with their footfalls. "I don't know. I'm just feeling confused. Are you picking up anything?" she muttered, trying to deflect the focus from herself.

Caroline looked at her with wide green eyes that reminded her so much of Elise. "No, just a headache. I feel totally blocked here." Behind them, following closely, were Max and Peter, occasionally murmuring to each other but largely silent.

The skin on the back of Cassie's neck prickled somewhere between irritation and awareness. And then there were the whispers, light feathery rushes around her ears. She couldn't be sure if they were real or if she was developing some inner ear infection that she had been oblivious to. All of it felt confusing. Many times, she'd begun to mention it, and then she stopped herself, feeling foolish.

Rick Lightner had stopped abruptly in front of a mammoth-sized, stainless steel gleaming stove, whirling around with a bit of flair. "Well, folks, not much more to see here. Just a kitchen, a big one, yes, but not much to recommend it," he laughed congenially.

"Aren't there tunnels?" Cassie murmured. Once again, she really hadn't meant to say that.

Rick looked at her a bit like she'd certainly lost her mind. "Tunnels, tunnels in the kitchen?"

"Yeah, Lightner, right on the other side of you." A tall, ebony-skinned man dressed in white, whom Cassie suspected was one of the chefs, had wandered up behind them.

"Oh, sorry folks, this is Joseph Montez, one of the assistant cooks here. And what were you saying, there are tunnels?"

"Yes," he chuckled openly at Lightner. "The Hotel Mandolin was designed with them — tunnels running throughout the building, connecting all the major areas. Just through those doors," he gestured.

Caroline tugged on her arm. "How did you know that, Mom?" Then her eyes met Peter Norfleet's. He looked at her with an expression that told her that she was now definitely the focus of his interest.

"So, these tunnels? You'd like to see them?" Rick Lightner inquired a bit dubiously.

"Yes," Max answered before anyone else spoke.

The mix had shifted a bit, and when exactly, she didn't know. But Lightner led the group, followed by Max, Caroline, Cassie, and Peter Norfleet, rounding out the party. She'd smiled at Peter once, but predominantly there were no words between them. Tension had settled amongst them all, and Cassie didn't have the energy to make small talk. She was too busy being overwhelmed by what she was feeling. The tunnel out of the kitchen was dubious at best. The floor was granite. The walls were regular sheetrock with a coat of gray paint that she suspected by the smell had been done rather recently, and of course, there was that somewhat musty scent of a place that was old in its construction. The ceiling wasn't particularly high but lined with pipes overhead.

It took a path that seemed to snake behind the kitchen. It led at one juncture onto a rather rudimentary set of stairs, then a narrow doorway heading to yet another flight of granite steps that Cassie swore ascended through several floors.

She breathed in deeply, steadying herself as they continued to climb. There was no handrail to grab, just the narrow flight of stairs. Beside her, Peter murmured again, "Are you all right?" That seemed to be his purpose today, periodically checking on her well-being. She wondered distractedly how dreadful she must look to inspire such concern.

"Yes, I'm not overly fond of such closed spaces," she murmured.

"Any idea where we're headed?" Max directed toward their guide.

"None whatsoever, quite the adventure," Lightner spat out jollily. And then they'd stopped at the top on a flat landing, no larger than three feet by three feet. Most of their group was still caught behind on the narrow granite stairs. "Ah, here we go," with a bit of force, Rick Lightner pushed through what appeared to be another doorway, allowing light to flood into the dimness of the narrow tunnel space.

Their group entered the light — an ornate, gleaming, tremendous, and empty room. Looking straight up, Cassie noted a stylized vaulted ceiling at least twenty feet high set off by half a dozen massive crystal chandeliers of unbelievably detailed artistry. And all of it was accented by an intricate-looking Grecian trim. "Ah, the ballroom," Lightner muttered.

Her head spun, emerging from such a confined space into the grandiose opulence and sheer massiveness of what was around her. But then she noticed Caroline separating from the group, wandering into the center of the room. "I know this. Don't you remember?" she said to Max.

"Yes," he answered with a concerned edge in his voice.

And then unexpectedly, Caroline suddenly put her hands over her eyes. "It's too much," she said in a panicked voice.

And Max was beside her, his arm around her. "I'm sorry, we have to leave." He said, already moving with Caroline to the hotel's main entrance to the ballroom.

"Yes, let's go," Cassie responded with concern, but behind her, in the open doorway, she continued to hear the soft whisper compelling her to stay.

A Late Night Drink

Five

"Are you sure you're all right?" Cassie asked.

They'd managed to make it into the hotel lobby, where Caroline was sitting next to her on an ornate camel-back, pink antique sofa. She still looked a bit too pale for Cassie's comfort. "Yes, I just started feeling overwhelmed, like I couldn't breathe. But it's better now. Max is going to take me somewhere to get some coffee so I can clear my head. You can come if you want," she murmured. And then it hit her rather abruptly. Caroline's mouth said you could come, but her eyes said she wanted to be alone to talk to Max. That was the way with them these days. They were living in a private world, talking in a secret language that no one else was privy to. And it wasn't that she minded much. She wanted her daughter to be happy. It just became a tad irritating at times.

"No, I think I'll take a cab home."

"Not at all. Let me take you." She again, for perhaps the hundredth time that evening, looked into the eyes of Peter Norfleet. She had no idea he'd been listening. "I don't want to cause you any inconvenience," she said carefully.

"Peter," he filled in with a curious smile. "No inconvenience Cassie," he answered.

She stood up, turning again to Caroline. "You're sure you'll be okay?" she asked.

And then Max chimed in, "Don't worry. I'll take care of her." She smiled, nodded, and bit her lip to stop uttering an ungenerous retort about how dismally well he'd taken care of her last spring.

"So, you seem very protective of your daughter."

She glanced up into those blue-gray eyes, wondering vaguely if she was being insulted. "Do I seem that way?"

He shrugged, "No criticism, just observation."

"Well, Mr. Norfleet."

He laughed, "Now you're really going to have to stop this Mr. Norfleet business."

"Oh, I'm sorry."

"Don't be. It's endearing, but it makes me feel like your accountant."

And just then, the waitress delivered two rather icy glasses filled with frozen margaritas. It had started with:

"Are you hungry?"

"No, I ate."

"Would you like coffee?"

"Well, maybe so."

"Would you rather a drink?"

"Well, I, yes, maybe so."

So, they'd ended up in a little café right on the more palatable end of Bourbon Street. Cassie had no idea why she'd said yes to a drink with Peter Norfleet. She was so fried. That was the only description that seemed to suit her, and beyond that, she didn't like feeling like a bunch of old luggage to be carted home while the kids went out to have fun. On the plus side, she really liked margaritas, although with the temperatures dropping outside, she realized perhaps it wasn't the smartest choice. In addition to all of this, as the evening progressed, more and more Peter Norfleet was looking like a slightly edgier James Brolin to her, and she didn't know why. But then again, maybe it was the being "fried" part of the equation.

Cassie smiled a bit sheepishly at the large frothy drink being placed in front of her. "Well, that looks good," she said, taking a sip. "I guess I worry about Caroline, not that it does any good."

"Because they do what they want anyway."

"Seems so," she murmured. Wow, this was no lightweight Margarita. It was pretty strong. "Do you have kids?"

"Yeah, a boy and a girl, a little older than your son."

"Oh," she murmured.

"Divorced."

"That couldn't have been fun," another sip, then she glanced at him. Was that the right thing to say in the situation? But he was smiling at her, seemed to soften that edginess a bit. "My husband died, well, when Caroline was a teenager. Jared was younger."

"That must have been difficult, raising the kids alone."

"I guess. I don't know. You just keep moving and do what you have to. I didn't think about it too much. My husband and I," then she stopped. Was she really going to divulge such private things?

He was stirring his frozen margarita with the tall straw they'd stuck in it. "Not close," he filled in.

She sighed, "That obvious?"

He glanced up at her. "I don't know, just a feeling."

"Well, Peter Norfleet, you may just be more psychic than you give yourself credit for."

He nodded, "How about some nachos with that drink?"

"Sounds decadent," she laughed.

"Yes, that might be my goal."

Peter let his instincts guide him. He'd stepped back, observing the events and then the reactions of the collective psychic party that Max Gravier had assembled at the Hotel Mandolin. He was an outsider in this cast of individuals. Admittedly, it had taken him some years to accept the validity of this line of inquiry completely, but he had. Experience and exposure to people like Max had taught him that there was far more going on in this world than the five senses suggested.

And given that, he felt, with his own set of sharpened instincts, that Cassie Breslin was a dark horse in the mix but also undeniably a key. She was the only one showing signs of connecting at any level to whatever was happening there. So, when the opportunity presented itself to spend some time alone with her, he seized on it. He would gain her confidence, then get her to confide her impressions.

So that was the plan. But here they were, sipping margaritas, enjoying lively conversation, and eating nachos. And he was getting a bit lost in the dreamy blue eyes of this beautiful woman. In truth, he had to struggle a bit at the moment to remember that there was a Hotel Mandolin.

"So, do you like living in the Warehouse district?"

"Love it."

"Really? I used to want to get an apartment in the French Quarter all by myself and paint."

"Are you an artist?" he asked.

She shook her head, "Not really, I dabble a bit. But it just always sounded so bohemian. I mean, living in the French Quarter."

"And that appealed to you?"

"On a level, shedding what I was, what I was expected to be and—"

"Taking on a different skin?" he murmured in a way that felt tantalizing to her.

She smiled, "Maybe." It was clear the drink had gone to her head. She wasn't censoring, not smart, but she didn't care.

"So," he began, "I've got to say that I'm really stuck on this case."

"The girl," she nodded. "Things didn't go as you'd hoped. Caroline didn't seem to pick up much of anything, or Max, it seems."

"But you did, didn't you, Cassie?" he said pointedly.

She glanced up slowly. Her eyes seemed so wide and oddly vulnerable now. "Why would you say that? I'm not a sensitive or really a psychic like Max?"

"I'm no expert, but maybe that's exactly why you could feel things there. You come at it on a different level. Did you sense anything?"

She paused, considering his question for a moment, and then considering how to frame an answer. "Honestly, what I felt was nearly overwhelming — almost crippling sadness."

"Sadness?" he echoed, considering her words. It had a ring of truth, what she'd said. He had felt sadness or what he'd interpreted as depression while they were inside the Mandolin. It was ephemeral, inconsistent, and truthfully, he'd attributed it purely to the morose state of mind he'd been carrying around for some time.

"You felt it too," she murmured, watching him intently with those intense eyes.

He frowned a bit. "I'm not sure. I suppose I attributed it to my feelings."

She smiled a bit pensively, "That's not unusual. I think a lot of people may do that who are more perceptive than they give themselves credit for. They just assume what they're feeling is a natural shift in their own emotions. They do this without examining any causality. I mean, really, is there a tangible reason that I am suddenly angry or afraid? If not, one should look outside oneself. Don't you think?" Cassie, still deeply lost in her train of thought, took another sip of her melting margarita. And not for the first time that evening, Peter Norfleet thought about kissing her. He thought perhaps the drink was going to her head the way she was speaking so openly to him. But then again, maybe she just liked him, he mused a bit indulgently.

"So, is it common for you to pick up these sorts of impressions?"

She opened her mouth as though to answer and then closed it again as though she had abruptly truncated that thought. Finally, after what seemed like an endless pause of consideration, she began to respond, "No, not really. I mean, I get impressions, but I'm better at simply focusing energy — to aid in healing, and actually, it's very helpful in gardening," she responded, her voice simply trailing off.

He'd felt a shift in her mood. Actually, it was her eyes. For some reason, he found them quite readable. "What's the matter Cassie?" he asked directly. It got him in trouble sometimes, his directness. His career, time as a cop, and afterward, had trained him that directness was unsettling to people. People being unsettled often helped him ferret out the truth. But as it was in more social circumstances, people preferred to be finessed, handled more gently — a skill he hadn't bothered to cultivate.

"I don't know. It was so strange that Max and Caroline couldn't pick up anything, strange that I did. It makes me question everything. Did I really feel anything? Or hear anything?"

"Hear?" he questioned, surprised as she hadn't mentioned it before.

"Oh, that's right. I'd forgotten. At times, I thought I heard things — people whispering at a distance."

"In the room?" he prodded.

"No," she said, shaking her head. "It was mostly the stairs and, of course, the tunnel, mostly there, I think."

He nodded, remembering sensations he was feeling in the old building, anxiety, uneasiness. "Any idea what was being said?"

"No, it was distorted. I couldn't make it out. Honestly, Peter, I can't say if it means anything."

"Well, maybe we should try to find out."

"Find out?"

"We should go back there again soon, I think."

Cassie checked her watch. It was after ten. She and Peter had spent quite a bit of time at the restaurant, time that had just seamlessly slipped by unnoticed. She tried not to puzzle this out too much, as was her nature. Raising her children virtually alone had made her a planner, not generally spontaneous. But tonight was different, unexpected, and she'd enjoyed herself — enjoyed talking and listening, having someone perceive her differently, not as a mother or a sister, but as an interesting person.

And she'd given him her phone number so they could hash out this plan of his to return to the Hotel Mandolin. Then he drove her home and walked her to her front door. She could feel a bit of a bizarre déjà vu — that tantalizing first date feeling, although clearly, this wasn't at all that, just two adults discussing ideas over drinks.

"Did you want to come in?" she asked spontaneously, somewhat to smooth the moment and not at all considering exactly how this would go if he said yes. They'd stopped in front of the heavy oak door at the entrance.

"No, I have some appointments in the morning."

She smiled, nodding, feeling a tad bit foolish. "Yes, it is getting late," she said.

"Cassie," he began, looking at her a bit intently. "I really enjoyed your company tonight."

"So, did I. Sorry we weren't of more help to you."

And when she thought this would be the end of it, he did something more than unexpected. Peter took one of her hands in his. "I was wondering if you'd have dinner with me tomorrow night."

It was unexpected and distracting. His hand over hers felt warm and charged. And she hadn't anticipated anything like this. "You mean to talk about the case," she said with distraction.

He smiled, "I meant I enjoyed spending time with you tonight and would like to do more of it. If that's all right?"

She felt the air go out of her chest a bit at his candidness. It wasn't an unpleasant sensation but unsettling, nonetheless. "All right, that would be nice."

"Pick you up at six?"

"Okay, that sounds fine."

His eyes hadn't left her face. But then he squeezed the hand he was still holding and slowly let it go. "Goodnight, Cassie," he said, quietly walking away into the darkness.

Her heart felt as though it was strumming a bit loudly in her chest when she opened the front door with her key. She'd felt a bit befuddled by the whole exchange. Maybe it was the margarita making her feel as though she didn't quite have her wits about her. But just as she entered the house, she was abruptly greeted by the rather grim faces of both Caroline and Jared sitting on the front of the staircase.

"Mom, where have you been?" Caroline asked in a rather stern voice.

"Why? Is it past my bedtime?"

Caroline stood up, arms crossed. "Max brought me home nearly an hour ago, and you weren't here."

"Yeah, where have you been?" Jared echoed, standing up, though in a little less accusatory tone.

She stared at both her children, feeling a bit of perverse pleasure at the tables being turned. "Peter and I went out for a drink."

"A drink?" Caroline echoed, a bit of the steel draining out of her voice.

"Yes, dear, any problem with that?"

Her daughter's face seemed to whiten ever so slightly. "No, I mean, I was surprised."

"Yeah, me too," she answered. "Now I'm going upstairs to bathe and then go to bed. Unless you two have any more questions."

Caroline was looking at her oddly. "No, we were just worried."

"Well," she smiled, "don't be. I'm plenty old enough to get myself out of my own messes. That is if I get into any."

The Lady in the Blue Dress

Six

The stairwell was narrow, narrow from the voluminous fabric of her evening gown. She leaned against the banister, staring down into the deep dark hole at the center of the staircase. The silk and velvet fabrics of her midnight blue dress had nearly caught on a small jagged piece of wood extending off the side of the stairs. If she had pulled harder, her garment would have snagged, and pulled even harder, she would have been caught in its folds, possibly lost her balance, and spilled down the staircase into that deep, dark center. And she wondered with distraction if there was silence down there, after the jolt, after life had been expelled. Was there silence? Quiet? Peace?

Cassie opened her eyes to the blackness of her room. She sat up in the bed, her heart pounding. Beside her, she opened a drawer of the white night table. She took out a pen and a small notebook and then wrote down the dream. There was no question in her mind that it was somehow very important.

"I don't know. It felt as though I was in her mind."

"The woman in the dream?"

"Yes, I was feeling what she was feeling."

Caroline put down her coffee cup, looking a bit concerned. "It sounds like a sort of empathic link. But that's unusual for you, Mom."

Cassie nodded, unusual, to put it lightly. She'd never experienced anything of this nature before. "I suppose it could have just been an imagining ignited by our time in the Mandolin."

"You've always said that it's important not to discount dreams."

"Yes, that's true." It was early morning, and Caroline was due at work in just a half hour. "It was definitely the stairs from the hotel. It did feel disturbing there."

"But this had nothing to do with Janie Tyler."

"No, no, it seemed long ago. The dress was long. But it was elaborate, formal with so much detailing — huge puffed sleeves, a small beaded waist, floor length. Antiquated, could have been the turn of the century."

"And the woman was contemplating suicide?"

Cassie sipped her coffee. Her head was pounding, and she was extremely anxious in just discussing this. Weirdly, it felt like a betrayal, like reading someone's diary. "It seems so," she murmured.

"I think we should talk to Max about this and maybe Peter."

"We're having dinner tonight."

She glanced up. Caroline was staring at her a bit intensely. "Really?" she said quietly.

"Yes, he asked me last night."

"And you said yes?"

Slowly, she put down her coffee cup. "I did. We seemed to have a bit of a rapport." Caroline continued to look at her strangely. "Is that a problem?"

Caroline shook her head, "No, not at all. He seems very nice."

"Yes, he is."

And then there was a slight smile on Caroline's face. "I'm glad, Mom. You deserve to have some fun."

"Well, we'll have to see if it's fun."

Caroline was off to work, Jared off to school, and it bothered her. Not being alone per se, but there was a feeling of uneasiness since the dream that seemed to have been cloaking her.

Cassie had tried a brief meditation. She'd settled in the turret room, her favorite room, mostly because she had claimed it entirely for herself. It was comfortable with lovely colorful chairs that she'd picked out and her own desk. Many mornings she would retreat here curled up on the sunny window seat, watching life go on around her on the busy Prytania Street below. At times she whimsically likened herself to the Lady of Shallot in her tower, simply observing life through its reflection in a mirror. Of course, she had no mirror and was abominable at knitting or any of the sewing arts, although her mother had tried to teach her. Eventually, she'd given up, *"Perhaps your strengths lay in other areas, my dearest one."* That was what she'd called her at times — *my dearest one*. But then again, she'd also called Elise my dearest one. It was strange. She'd always felt her mother a bit more protective of Elise because she seemed different and thus more vulnerable. But Cassie hadn't felt jealous. Instead, she'd also become protective of Elise, which of course, didn't sit very well with Elise. She'd always been determined to live on her terms, regardless of how others perceived it.

Cassie had lit candles in the room and pulled the shades on its windows. When she and Allen had first moved into the house, they'd left the turret room largely unoccupied. He'd found it too small for his office, and Cassie was so absorbed in their, or rather his, plans for the rest of the house that she'd left it untouched. She'd vaguely thought of a playroom for the children once they arrived, but that idea had drifted away. And then Allen died so unexpectedly. It was his heart, an undetected problem that became exacerbated into a massive coronary. They'd told her that it couldn't have been predicted. So, in an instant, life changed.

She closed her eyes, trying to push away the memories, but today they seemed determined to come in a flood.

All of it had been such a shock, a jolt that was effective.

She woke up.

It's curious to realize that you've been living in a bit of a fog, simply from moment to moment. Plans, yes, but superficial ones like what to fix for dinner or how to arrange a party. Not the ones that really count. Like, am I happy? What purpose does my life serve? What do I want?

Maybe it had been easier not to ask such questions. Maybe she'd kept herself busy enough with the kids, Allen, and the house that she didn't need to ask herself these things. And then a bucket of ice-cold water was splashed against her consciousness, and she slowly began asking and was still asking.

Again, she attempted to clear her mind, breathing in deeply as the toxic recollections began to squirm away like scurrying mice.

She focused on a peaceful place, a serene lake where she pictured herself sitting calmly on its banks. Breathe in the positive. Breathe out the negative. She coached herself.

Then surprisingly, she felt her mind being pulled, nearly yanked elsewhere.

Again, she was on the staircase at the great hotel, leaning over its banister. But it wasn't her. It was someone else. She breathed deeply, and her skin ached with an onslaught of irritation.

"Margaret, Margaret," she heard her name called, and she looked upward into the face of a man with cruel black eyes.

Cassie's eyes snapped open. She'd felt a pain lodge right into her heart. She was breathing deeply, rapidly, something akin to panic.

She blew out the candles and left the room on shaking limbs.

In the aftermath, being in the house all alone felt creepy in a way that she'd never experienced before. She needed to get out but had no idea where to go. Shakily, she headed into the kitchen for some water. Her hand was actually trembling when she took the bottle out of the refrigerator.

She put it down on the counter, willing herself to calm down. And then, rather inopportunely, nearly making her jump out of her skin, her cell phone went off with that bizarre rap ringer that Jared had put on it as a joke. She stilled herself, although she had the strongest inclination to smash the thing to the floor.

"Hello," she answered, not bothering to check who it was.

"Cassie, it's Peter. Is this a bad time?" he asked a bit carefully, clearly picking up on the strangeness of her tone.

"No, no," she said shakily. "It's the perfect time."

The Investigator

Seven

She felt foolish. But she desperately didn't want to be in the house alone. Peter had heard it succinctly in her voice, the shakiness, perhaps the fear. Was she feeling fear? Cassie wasn't sure. She was enormously rattled, and for her, that was unusual. She was usually the steady one, the dependable one that would dispatch horrible insects and even a mouse or two when the kids were young. Then again, that was mainly because Allen simply wasn't around. And, of course, she'd been exposed to plenty of phenomena in the psychic realm courtesy of her sister and children.

But this had gotten to her — the terror she'd felt, or that woman had felt, on the staircase. It was disturbing. The way her feelings, whoever she was, had become linked, intertwined, with Cassie's. So now she was waiting out on the back porch, waiting for Peter Norfleet to rescue her, from what exactly she had no clue.

She was sitting on the glider when he turned the corner and ascended the steps to the screen door of the porch. She'd told him to meet her out here. She couldn't bear to be inside the house a second longer. It felt disturbing, as though she'd let something potentially threatening in there.

As he opened the door, Cassie smiled at him, feeling a bit ridiculous. Peter wore a sports coat, beige shirt, and khaki pants, dressed in different clothes but not all that different from the first time he'd come to the house. "Peter, I'm sorry. You shouldn't have had to come all the way here."

He sat down beside her on the glider, looking at her thoughtfully. "You sounded pretty upset."

"I'm all right," she said, feeling it hit her ears rather hollowly.

He took her hand in his, just as he'd done last night. "Okay, that doesn't seem to be true. What happened exactly?"

She shook her head, "I don't know. I think I've tapped into something."

"Something from the hotel?" he said grimly.

"Yes, I think so."

And then he squeezed her hand reassuringly. "Tell me."

Peter walked around the turret room of Cassie Breslin's house. This was where she'd had the vision of the woman on the stairwell and the malevolent man with her. He wasn't a psychic, and he knew what he could do was limited. But this space afforded him an unusual feeling, of a sort of sanctuary, for Cassie — undeniably a distinctly feminine space, although it wasn't particularly flowery or delicate. It had that vibe, a private place where perhaps the masculine presence wasn't encouraged.

"So, this woman is the same one from the dream?"

"Seems so," she murmured. She was sitting behind the large cherry wood desk, looking very distracted.

Peter continued pacing the rather limited, round space, trying to whittle out the facts if there were indeed any facts here. "And you feel as though she is real, a person?"

She shook her head, "I don't know, Peter. All I know is that she was contemplating throwing herself down the stairwell."

"Suicide, like Janie Tyler?"

"I," she hesitated, "I hadn't thought about that. I mean, yes. It would be suicide, but different, of course."

He nodded, staring out the window momentarily into the street below. "Yes, different," he said coolly, "but still suicide. And the woman's name—"

"Margaret, he called her Margaret. She seemed terrified of him."

Peter turned, staring at Cassie. "Well, I think we need to find out if there ever was a Margaret and if she or anyone else ever fell down that stairwell."

"It seemed like a long time ago. She was in a long dress."

He stared at her, considering, "I'll have to check back when the Hotel Mandolin first opened."

"Do you think there's anything to this?"

"It's a thread, a thread worth pursuing. Will anyone be home soon?" he asked.

Cassie shook her head, "No, Caroline won't be in until after five and Jared sometime after."

"Well, I have things to do. Why don't you come along with me?"

She stood up, again feeling a bit ridiculous. "Look, I don't need a babysitter."

He smiled, "Come on. I'll enjoy your company. And I'll buy you lunch. Besides, I'm not leaving you alone until we understand what we're dealing with."

She sighed. He was quite determined. This was evident, but not in an unpleasant way. And she was willing to go along with him. There was still something here that she was feeling on her skin. "I just need to change," she said, heading through the doorway.

"I'll wait," she heard him say behind her.

And he did buy her lunch at another interesting little restaurant nestled deep inside the River Bend section of the city, just where St. Charles Avenue intersected with Carrollton Avenue. It was a small, primarily Italian restaurant with a private courtyard that, as time went on, began to fill up quite substantially. "I've never been to this place before," she commented as the waitress headed from the courtyard back into the building with their order.

"Well, I've spent a lot of time canvassing the city. Needless to say, I know it pretty well," he said with a quick smile.

Slipping into his world was pleasantly disorienting. It felt faster, more textured, slicker if she might even use that word without trepidation. Of course, they lived in the same city, but in most ways did not really live in the same city. This she was discovering. Peter Norfleet didn't look at people as she did and didn't operate with the inherent trust that this insulated widow seemed to take for granted. For him, life was a place of shadows where people weren't granted the benefit of the doubt. Instead, they were granted the mantle of distrust until they earned something different.

"You've been quiet. Still upset?" he asked.

They'd spent a strange morning traveling all over New Orleans proper, stopping by the police station, the dry cleaners, a bar uptown that was open quite early, and The New Orleans Public Library. Here Peter had started searching for the mysterious Margaret, who might or might not have come to an untimely end at the Mandolin.

"I thought all those death records had been put on computer."

"Some, but there are gaps. If I want to be thorough, I like to have a look at the originals. The library has quite a collection from the coroner's office."

"And the library—"

"Has quite a collection as well as people who know how to use them to their greatest advantage."

So, she'd tagged along and watched Mr. Norfleet move seamlessly through a landscape that intrigued her.

Lilian McCauley, a woman a good ten years her senior, had greeted him with cordiality.

She was a prim, well-dressed, silver-haired woman who seemed to light up like a Christmas tree at the prospect of digging up some elusive mystery from the past.

"And nothing but Margaret?"

"Yes, but definitely connected to the Mandolin. May have died there in its early days."

"Really? Not much to go on, Pete," she murmured, her eyes narrowing just a notch.

"Yeah, but I thought if you could just look at any early deaths, maybe 1880s to 1910 or 1920s."

"Hmm," she expelled a bit, scribbling notes on a yellow legal tablet. "May take a while. Death certificates aren't generally categorized by place of expiration."

"Well, whatever you can do, Lil, I'd appreciate."

She nodded, her eyes passing quickly over Cassie and then back to Peter. "Can you tell me what this is all about?"

He smiled in a way that Cassie sensed Lilian McCauley seemed to appreciate. "Not yet. It's too early."

"I'm sorry. What did you say?" Cassie asked. Her mind had floated far afield from this lovely courtyard in the Riverbend.

Peter smiled at Cassie, but it was different. Not that smile that said he was trying to get something out of you, just one that spoke of curiosity. "You're preoccupied."

"I am sorry, just trying to absorb a lot of stuff. Wondering if all of this is something I've conjured up in my imagination."

"I'm wondering, Cassie," he said rather deliberately. "What's making you doubt yourself so much?"

His comment felt like a bit of an unpleasant jolt. "Um, I don't know. This feels like uncharted territory for me."

"Not the psychic thing?"

"No," she said, then rethought, "Yes, maybe, these impressions are different from anything I've experienced, and they're ephemeral, weak, and so intangible. And yes, I doubt them."

"That vision you described didn't seem all that weak."

She took a sharp breath as it flashed across her mind again, the woman in the blue dress, the fear she'd felt. "No, I suppose not. I don't know." She glanced up at him. He watched her with those intense eyes as though he was trying to dig behind what she was saying to get to the truth. "Do you really like your life?" He smiled at the abrupt shift, and immediately she realized how rude that must sound. "I'm sorry."

"Why?" he asked, genuinely seeming a bit amused.

"I guess that sounded invasive."

"It sounded strange. Do I like my life? Well, sometimes and sometimes not, I suppose." She nodded, taking a sip of the glass of water that was in front of her. "So, what did you mean by that question?"

She looked up, wondering indeed what she meant. "I don't know. I guess I meant being suspicious of everyone all the time. It seems like life is just filled with suspects for you."

"Instead of relationships?"

"No," she said instinctively as her well-bred manners demanded she do. "I mean. It just seems like a different way to live."

"Well, it is. And I don't find everyone to be a suspect. You aren't," he responded thoughtfully.

"I'm not?"

He shook his head. "No, I find you very genuine and charming."

She laughed, "And too benign to be a threat to anyone."

"No, no, I wouldn't go that far," he said a bit more softly.

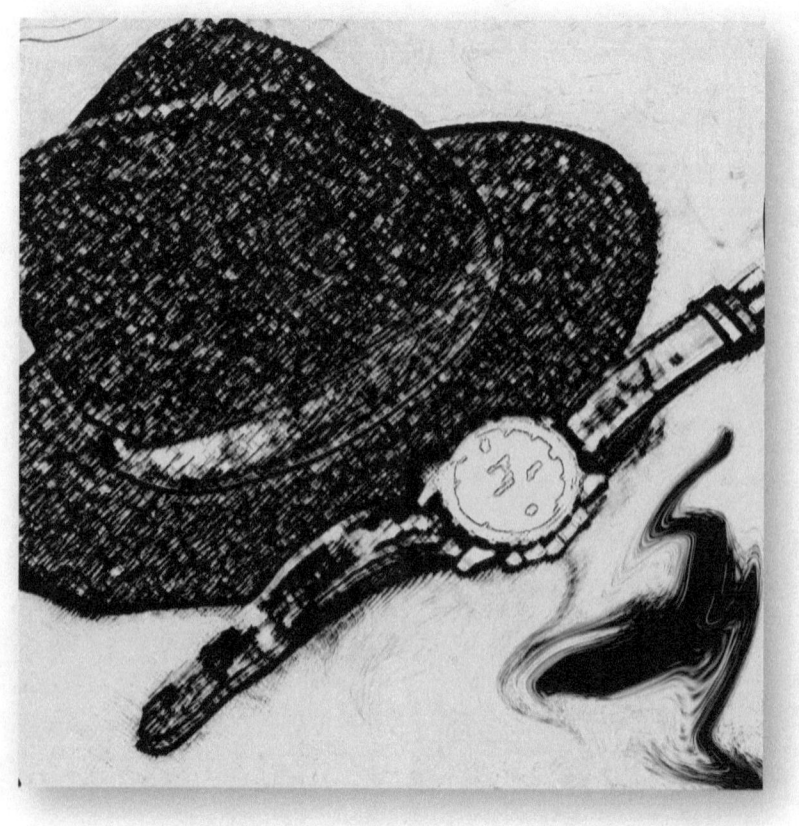

A Link

Eight

"There's nothing here," Caroline murmured.

She and Max had made a second pass through the house, focusing most particularly on Cassie's turret room.

"Are you certain?" Cassie asked, with a bit of confusion in her voice. Both of them had spent time walking from room to room in the house, trying to unearth something that might explain Cassie's vision. She'd spent the balance of the afternoon with Peter, and then they'd returned to the house. Upon hearing her story, Caroline called Max.

Max shook his head slowly, "I'm sorry, Cassie. Whatever you've locked onto isn't centered here."

"Mom, didn't you say the vision took place at that hotel?" Jared said.

"Yes," Cassie agreed rather softly.

"Max, any idea why you and Caroline can't seem to pick anything up on this?" Peter asked.

"None. I don't really understand it."

Cassie nodded, feeling slightly deflated and sinking onto the tapestried window seat. "Unless it's in my mind."

"I didn't say that, Mom," Caroline comforted, sitting beside her.

"Well, how else can we explain it? This isn't even my area, these visions, and none of you are experiencing anything like it."

"There may just be an explanation," Max said a bit grimly. "One we just haven't figured out yet."

"She was quite upset this morning. She didn't want to stay in the house alone."

"That seems a bit unusual for Cassie. I mean, she's always struck me as very even-keeled, albeit very protective of her children."

Peter and Max had walked outside the house to hash things out. "Something's gotten to her, and it's tied in with our visit to the Mandolin."

Max sighed a bit. "And you want Cassie to go back there."

"Maybe," he murmured. "Sometimes it's best to meet things head-on."

"Even before you have any idea what you are facing?"

"You need to wait for Aunt Elise. She's more equipped to deal with this kind of phenomenon."

"She won't be home for another several weeks. I'm not sure whatever it is will keep."

"Promise me, Mom. Promise you'll try to wait."

"Caroline, I'm not a child, nor am I foolish. Maybe it will all blow over."

Caroline was staring at her with her sister's wide green eyes, which told her succinctly that she wasn't convinced.

Cassie had walked Peter to the front door. It was approaching six, and she was already battling a raging headache from all the day's strangeness. "I'm sorry about dinner and taking up all your time today."

"Well, I'll take a rain check on dinner, and I must admit that I enjoyed having my time tied up with you today."

She smiled, "You're being gallant."

"I'm being honest. But I need you to promise to call me if anything else happens or you need someone to listen to you."

She hesitated as he took her hand in his. This was something he was becoming quite comfortable doing. "All right, I will. You seem the only one in this bunch not trying to tell me what I should do."

"I'm sure you're the best judge of that."

"Yes, well, you would think so."

And then he leaned in, giving her a quick kiss on the cheek before he left. She watched him walk to his car. Her heart was still beating faster as she'd thought for a moment that he would kiss her on the mouth. And she wondered pleasantly how she would have reacted.

Cassie breathed deeply and paced the length of her room. Perhaps she shouldn't have canceled dinner with Peter tonight. She was climbing out of her skin. It would have been a distraction. He was, and she hesitated decidedly a most intriguing distraction. No, not exactly. An enigma, maybe? She glanced at the clock, going on eleven.

Caroline had wanted her to call Elise, call Elise in France.

"Really, in France?"

"We could use Skype."

"Isn't this a bit of an overreaction?"

"You didn't want to be alone in your house today."

And then the subject was dropped, dropped like a lead balloon. She shook her head, allowing her blonde locks to fly around her head in disarray.

This had to stop. She had to get a grip.

She sat up on her queen-sized bed and pulled the pillows straight behind her back. She really needed to start taking those yoga classes again. There were way too many aches and pains. She breathed deeply and closed her eyes, clearing her mind.

In her thoughts, she whispered *guide me to inner peace* and then felt a fluttering of energy within her situated around her solar plexus. Another deep cleansing breath, and she focused more intently on a white energy flooding throughout her.

It was good, steadying, calming to her. Her focus expanded until she felt something, not unlike a soft belt wrapping around her waist. Then abruptly shattering the calmness, it clamped fiercely around her in a tight grip.

Before she could disengage, she felt her consciousness fiercely yanked to another place.

She breathed in deeply, but this time the air felt cold, icy in its texture.

"Where am I?" the thought was propelled outward but somehow snuffled out in a cacophony of other sounds.

It was overwhelming — the cold, the cold surrounding her, inside of her, her skin, her breath, all of it.

She moved down a long, narrow hallway that seemed it might be a corridor of rooms at the hotel. But it was insubstantial, mutating at times — seeming modern with the walls as she remembered them beige with the lower half a black and gold paisley sort of design. And then it melted into something else, a delicate pattern of wallpaper covering the whole wall, floral with graduating shades of light green and silver.

It was impossible to think. She was smothered. A humid weight dragged her down as she attempted movement. It was heavy, too heavy, the blue velvet dress that dragged along the floor. It had increased in weight as though it were drenched in water.

Thoughts, muffled thoughts, tried to penetrate the fog.

"Must be quiet, must be."

But she dragged on, the heavy dress, making a scraping sound as she walked. She ached, ached all over, her muscles tired and cumbersome.

Then stopping, she was on the stairwell again, staring straight down into that black hole that felt clearly as though it was reaching up to engulf her.

Cassie opened her eyes, shivering violently. She pulled herself out of bed and ran to the basin in her bathroom. Her face was pale, and her hair drenched in sweat. She turned on the cold water and splashed it again and again on her face. She didn't stop until she was sure she was grounded in this world and not the one that poor pathetic creature existed in.

"Maybe Max could come to stay here for a while."

Cassie frowned. What little sleep she'd gotten after her derailed meditation had left her in a foul and agitated mood. Her dreams had been filled with disjointed and disconnected images, all centered within the Hotel Mandolin. Something had seeped into her consciousness from that place, something that was beginning to drive her a little nuts. She paced across the kitchen with her cup of coffee slightly sloshing onto the floor with her sharp movements. "Do you really think Max being here will drive away all the gremlins?" she snapped a bit.

Caroline's face looked a bit stoic at her response. Clearly, she'd hurt her feelings, and she hadn't meant to. But she'd been on her own long enough to know that the presence of some man wouldn't fix everything. She'd learned that rather quickly after she was first married. She couldn't depend on Allen, not the way she'd assumed she would be able to. She'd been foolish and stupid and knew what she was feeling had a hundred percent to do with her and very little to do with her daughter's relationship. Max Gravier was a different sort of man than Caroline's father had been. But that being said, she still wasn't confident that he could fix whatever was happening here.

"I'm sorry, Cara. I'm in a terrible mood today. I don't believe trying to hide from whatever is happening is the way to fix things."

"Then what do you want to do?"

She stared at her, a bit dumbfounded — excellent question. What exactly did Cassie Breslin want to do about this?

And at that moment, almost in response, her cell phone rang that awful tune that she, almost more than anything, needed Jared to change. "Hello."

"Cassie, it's Peter. How was your night?"

Caroline, who had been staring straight at her, dropped her large green eyes down to her coffee cup. "Pretty bad, I'd have to say."

There seemed to be a pause on the line. "I'm sorry to hear that. Well, my contact at the New Orleans Public Library turned up some information for us more quickly than I'd expected. I was going to drop by, but not if you're not up to it."

She shook her head, "No, that would be good. I'll put on a fresh pot of coffee."

"See you in about twenty minutes."

"Good," and then she hung up without saying goodbye. She was beyond scrambled this morning. She glanced over to the breakfast table, where Caroline's eyes were on her again. "Peter is coming over. He's dug up some information about the hotel."

"That's good," Caroline said. "I'd like to hear it."

"What about work?" Cassie asked.

"I'll be late," her daughter replied with steel in her voice.

Margaret Monjure

Nine

They all sat around Cassie's little breakfast nook — she, Caroline, Jared, who Caroline had dragged out of bed, although his classes weren't until noon today, and Peter. And to his credit, Peter seemed perfectly calm and unfazed by the amount of scrutiny focused on him, while Cassie, in contrast, literally felt as though she was peeling out of her skin. She had no business drinking another cup of coffee, but that concrete realization didn't stop her.

"Well, my friend Lilian McCauley up at the public library managed to turn up more than a bit of information about the Mandolin. I suppose I should have looked at this angle before, given my investigation into Janie Tyler's death, but honestly, I hadn't considered it."

"What angle?" Caroline asked quickly.

Peter glanced over to Cassie, but she just continued to slowly stir the sugar into her coffee. It was something she'd been doing for far past its duration of usefulness. "Is it Margaret?" she asked softly.

"Part of it, I suppose. There was a record of a Margaret Monjure's death at the hotel around 1908."

"Suicide?" Cassie asked, anticipating a confirmation.

But Peter looked at her strangely, "No, actually murder, she was strangled in her room."

Cassie straightened up in her chair, a bit dumbfounded by that revelation. "Strangled? Really?"

"According to a coroner's account, but it does get stranger. A Henri Monjure, Margaret's husband, was also found dead."

"Murdered too?" Caroline asked.

"It's not certain. He fell in the stairwell, found on the ground floor as though he fell right over the railing into the center."

"The black hole," Cassie whispered.

"What did you say, Mom?" Jared asked, looking at her as if she'd gone off the deep end.

"Something from a dream, so they don't know if his death was a murder or not?"

"Neither was solved." He said a bit flatly, watching her with his inquisitive eyes, looking she thought for something she was not saying.

"What did you mean about there being an angle?"

"Yeah, well, we piqued Lilian's curiosity, so she continued digging. She found that there had been twenty deaths there since 1908, not including the Monjures'."

She shook her head, trying to soak up what he was saying. "Twenty, do you mean including natural causes?"

"No, I'm sorry, Cassie. I should have clarified twenty, including murders and suicides only. And out of the twenty, sixteen were classified as suicides up to Janie Tyler."

She stared at him a bit non-believing, "Sixteen," she whispered, finding it difficult to comprehend what she had heard.

"I don't know, Mom. This is getting more than bizarre. Maybe you should wait for Aunt Elise."

They'd moved into the den, both her children becoming quite agitated at her silence, but her mind was whirling. Margaret hadn't fallen down that stairwell. Her husband, Henri Monjure, had. Was he the man threatening her, or was it someone else entirely? And then, on top of it, the suicides. Why so many in such a concentrated space? "Peter, what do you think of all of this?"

He'd been quiet, letting Caroline and Jared verbally hash things out. "I'm not a paranormal expert, but in my line of work, I never chalk things up to coincidence. More often than not coincidence is much rarer than things being linked in some obscure way."

She nodded, feeling, feeling a flurry of things. "I need to go back to that hotel."

Caroline's eyes widened, "Mom, you don't know what you'd be getting into there. People are dying at an alarming rate."

"Margaret is in trouble."

"Margaret is dead," Caroline exploded.

"That doesn't mean she doesn't need help. She's reaching out to me. I know that — the dreams, the meditations."

Caroline unexpectedly turned to Peter. "Tell her this is not a good idea."

Peter Norfleet looked at both of them as though considering carefully. "I'm sorry. I can't. We need to confront this head-on."

Caroline, wide-eyed with panic, then looked to her brother. "Jared!"

He shrugged, curiously calm in the face of his sister's mounting hysteria. "Mom's right. Whatever it is, it is coming here now. We might as well go after it where it lives."

Caroline stared at him in disbelief. "I'm calling Max," she said, marching out of the room.

"Yeah, Max saves the world these days," Jared mumbled.

"Your sister is just on edge. She has been ever since—"

"Yeah, I know," Jared said, cutting her off a bit.

"What do you want to do?" Peter asked.

She sighed, "Pack a bag, I think. So, I can spend a few nights in the Hotel Mandolin."

Jared stood up, "Look, Mom, despite what I said, you can't do this alone."

"She won't be alone," Peter said rather curtly. Cassie smiled at him but wondered exactly what he meant. Did he intend to share a hotel room with her while she was ensconced at the Hotel Mandolin?

Ghosts

Ten

It was getting complicated, but then again, nothing was particularly unusual about that, given the psychic strain running through her family. So, as it was, they had a room on the fifth floor, not 503, where Janie Tyler died, but instead 515. Instead, she and Caroline had room 515, and Peter, Max, and Jared had the adjoining room 517. Jared had seemed more inclined to bunk in with the men. She and Peter had arrived at two in the afternoon to check-in, and the remaining bulk of their party would join them around six thirty after Max closed his shop. She had no idea if this arrangement would work. Her kids would be filtering in and out as work and school schedules allowed, and Cassie and Peter would be muddling around the hotel during the day unless, of course, he had another case to attend to. That was possible. She had no idea, but they were determined to protect her from whatever lurked in this posh and elegant old establishment. And she appreciated their concern, at least, she thought she did.

There was a light tap on the adjoining door between the two rooms. Opening it, Peter walked in, seeming a bit amused. "All settled in?" he asked.

"Yes, enjoying the quiet, of course, it's not going to last."

He sat on the edge of one of the two double size beds. "Well, I think it's great how protective your family is of you. So many families aren't so close."

"I suppose," she sighed, "but sometimes it makes me feel as though they think I'm incapable of handling things."

"Oh, I doubt that," he said softly. "These are extraordinary circumstances."

"I guess so," she answered, glancing around the room speculatively. Now that they were here, she had no clue where to begin.

"Problem?" he asked.

"Honestly, I'm not sure where to start."

"Well, why don't we take a walk around the hotel, get a feel for the lay of the land?"

She nodded, "As good an idea as any I have."

It seemed quiet. At least, that was what Cassie picked up on roaming through the hallways of the Mandolin. There was nothing obvious, nor was it a natural feeling. There was something muffled about the energy of the place, something — how could she put it — unreadable.

"Are you okay?" Peter Norfleet inquired as they wandered out the doors of the fourth floor. It was a bit like a secretive nook, surrounded on the sides by parts of the building. Nestled on a flat roof within was a lovely patio and the Olympic-size swimming pool, now concealed with a tarp.

"Yes," she answered, breathing in deeply the cool air around them. It was better out here, better than the odd staleness within. "Don't you have other cases you should be working on?"

"Probably, but I'm a bit of a night owl. I brought my laptop. Thought I'd find some odd spot in the hotel to do some work while everyone else is sleeping."

She stopped near some poolside lounge chairs that had been left out and decided to settle in for a moment. They had been consistently walking around the hotel for the last half hour. Peter sat in the chair across from her, seeming distracted. "You can function on such a lack of sleep?"

"Seems like the older I get, the easier it becomes."

She glanced around the deserted area. Evidently, this poolside deck had little draw for anyone else than them in the autumn. "What time is it?" she asked.

"About four."

She nodded, feeling more than a bit despondent. "I was hoping—"

"That this would be quickly resolved," he offered.

"Before all the other experts converged."

He laughed, "That's what they are, experts?"

"I don't know. I guess that's not fair. It's just that you raise children, spend so much time making decisions for them when they're growing up. And then all of a sudden, when you're not paying attention, they decide they have the right to tell you what to do."

"Ah, grown up and all."

"Yes, I suppose. But while they're growing up, I didn't become the child, you know."

"They're protective."

He leaned back in his lounge chair, putting his feet up. "I suppose it's different for a man. You see them growing up and then see them drifting away with their own lives. Being divorced and all gives one a different perspective."

"You feel like an outsider," she murmured.

"Often, maybe it's my fault. Although I tried to stay involved, but once Melinda remarried, well, they were busy, all of them, forging a new life."

"I'm sorry." She could feel the pain in his voice, although it was well concealed beneath his easy-going veneer.

"It's life. Change is inevitable."

"I suppose," she said. "And we simply have to let go of how things used to be."

"And see what evolves."

She closed her eyes momentarily, leaning back more comfortably in the lounge chair. "You have a habit of finishing my thoughts."

"Sorry, it seems easy for me to feel where they're going."

"That's strange," she said just before a wave of sleepiness hit her, a wave so strong that she felt herself falling asleep before even warning Peter it was happening.

It was powerful.

Her hands were touching the wall, a cold wall with so little light. It was rough on her palms, but somehow it was also comforting, feeling the texture. She continued to walk, pulling her long skirt. She knew the heavy material was already ripped in places, worn down, faded, and her body hurt so much. But she continued to move forward deep within the tunnel, although it was almost in darkness.

"Margaret," she heard him calling, dragging his broken, mangled body after her, just to put his cold hands on her throat again — squeezing her throat again until she couldn't breathe. She leaned against the coldness of the wall, and it was wet, dripping. But she couldn't see. It was too dark.

"Margaret," he called, almost like a plaintive wail in the darkness.

And she sunk against the cold, wet stone onto the floor, collapsing against it, waiting, trembling, hiding in the shadows.

Cassie opened her eyes. She was sitting up straight in the chair but still feeling hands directly on her throat, squeezing the breath from her.

Peter was standing over her, grasping her shoulders. "Cassie, what's wrong?"

She could still feel it, the woman lying against the cold, sticky wall in the dark, as though it were her. But then it wasn't. He shook her as though to bring her focus back to him. "Come on, Cassie," he said, crouching before her. "It was a dream."

She drew a deep breath focusing, focusing on his voice. It was leaving. Slowly, the mist she was wrapped in was leaving. "Okay," she whispered. Her voice sounded hoarse in her ears, as it would sound if someone had tried to crush her windpipe.

Peter insisted rather inflexibly that she return to her room, and they wait for her children and Max to arrive. And given the way she was feeling, Cassie offered no argument. "Do you want some more water?" he asked with concern.

She swallowed. Her throat was still sore. It was odd, at least in her experience, for a dream to have such a physical manifestation. "I don't think so," she said.

Peter nodded and crossed to the window in the room, staring outside for perhaps the hundredth time since they'd arrived. Cassie was sitting in a chair near the bed. She didn't want to lie down. Another dream like that one could just be more than she could stand. "We may have made a mistake here, jumping into this," he said softly but with a definitive note of strain in his voice.

"I don't know," she said, actually feeling the need to be reassuring to him, although she was the one who had gone through the jarring dream or vision. She couldn't quite decide which one it was. "I can't shake the feeling that Margaret's husband murdered her. What was his name?"

"Henri, Henri Monjure."

"I could feel her fear of him. It felt like she was in the tunnels hiding from him."

"But Margaret Monjure wasn't found in the tunnels. She was found in her room."

Cassie swallowed again on a sore lump in her throat that didn't want to go away. She turned away from Peter's face, trying to mentally focus again on what she'd

71

seen in the dream, what she'd felt. "I don't know. I know it was her, and she was there, in those tunnels. But they were different, coarser, rougher, and sticky. I couldn't be sure, but it seemed like there was blood, blood on the walls."

"Blood?" he said a bit sharply. "Cassie, there wouldn't be blood in a strangulation."

Her eyes widened. He was right. None of this was adding up. Again, she forced herself to remember the horrifying details. She remembered the pain around Margaret's throat, the crushing pain as though she had already been strangled. She had felt the impression of hands, strong hands crushing the air out of her. Her body had been weak, languid, and the dress. She stopped. Now she remembered. The dress had been torn, dirty, fading in places, deteriorating. And that sound, that sound she was running from. "Margaret, he'd said," she nearly whispered.

"Henri?" Peter asked.

"I, I think so," Cassie was trying hard to focus, trying so hard to see it again. She could feel him following her, but dragging, shuffling, as though his body had been damaged as well. "Oh God," she said, the realization suddenly crashing in on her.

"What?"

She looked up at Peter with almost confusion. "I was wrong. What I've been tapping into isn't the past at all. It's now."

"Now? I really don't understand."

"Margaret and Henri Monjure are ghosts, ghosts haunting the Mandolin."

Negative Energy

Eleven

Max Gravier was beginning to feel a bit concerned. He was increasingly uncomfortable with the way things were unfolding at the Hotel Mandolin. There were the strange visions Cassie Breslin seemed to be experiencing at an increasingly rampant pace, as well as the long string of suicides that Peter Norfleet's researcher had uncovered. And on top of that, and in some ways even more disturbing to him, was the odd stringent mood he found Caroline in when he arrived.

This whole business was taking a peculiar toll on her. She was edgy, overly emotional, and basically off-kilter at times.

"So, you believe this is a haunting of some sort?" he asked Cassie while keeping Caroline and all her reactions within the periphery of his vision.

"It seems so," she said. "All the impressions and visions I'm experiencing seem to be taking place in that odd sort of reality that spirits construct around themselves when they haven't crossed over."

"Odd sort of reality? Sorry, you've lost me," Peter interjected.

They'd all convened in Cassie and Caroline's hotel room at the Hotel Mandolin, where Cassie had rather calmly informed them of the latest developments.

Max had thought to explain, but before he could, Cassie directly began to answer Peter's question. "When someone dies in a traumatic way, suicide being the most jarring way a spirit can experience death, they often become confused for a time — trapped in the earthly plane and unable to move onto a more spiritual dimension."

"So, we are speaking of ghosts," Peter said.

Max watched the interplay between them closely, speaking to each other in a manner that made him feel a bit as though he wasn't even in the room. "Yes, though I hate to use this term. But for them, it's a kind of insanity, the entity not thinking clearly. They're trying to reconnect with a physical life they can't reach anymore, and within their perception, reality becomes convoluted and warped."

Max sat down slowly on the edge of the bed, feeling a bit useless. He glanced over to Caroline, who was standing across the room. Her eyes were wide, fixed on her mother, and he could feel something odd around her. It was quite odd, almost like a layer of negative energy enveloping her. "Max, have you run across this kind of thing before?" Peter asked.

The question shook him a bit. He was so caught up in his observations. "Yes, there are a lot of hauntings around here in a city as old as New Orleans. Some of these lost souls can be helped, but others are too caught up in their self-created drama that they are not open to receiving aid." And then he tacked on almost as an afterthought, "Of course, some things simply won't happen until it is the proper time."

"I think that's what is happening here. I mean with Margaret and perhaps Henri Monjure. They are ghosts, and I think he killed her," Cassie stated emphatically.

"So why would she be so trapped? She wasn't culpable in anything, didn't kill him, and didn't kill herself. Why is she trapped?" It was Jared who had been content to listen quietly but now cut in with a bit of chilling, concise logic that Max felt grateful for.

"I don't know," Cassie whispered. "I guess we don't understand everything."

"And all those other people," Caroline murmured strangely. "Those people who are killing themselves. What does that have to do with any of this?"

Cassie looked at her daughter with a bit of surprise, as if she were now picking up on the strange vibes from her that Max had been feeling. "I don't know, Caroline."

"Maybe, just maybe, you should figure it out, figure it out before you go jumping any deeper into this."

Cassie stood up from the chair that she'd been sitting in. "Caroline, what's the matter with you?"

Caroline was almost glaring at her but at the same time rubbing her arms a bit frantically as though there was some physical irritation on her. "I don't know. I feel like I'm crawling out of my skin here."

Max walked closer to her, feeling the bad energy all over her now as though it were a tangible thing. "Something's getting to you. You might need to leave."

"I'm not leaving here," her voice had risen in volume and pitch. "Do you think I will leave my mother in all this craziness with people killing themselves here? You don't know when I was young."

"Caroline," Cassie snapped, clearly to silence her.

Caroline's eyes widened a bit. "Oh, sorry, I forgot I'm not supposed to talk about it."

"It has no bearing."

Caroline let out a short laugh that Max found didn't sound like her in the least. "It has no bearing? People are killing themselves here. We don't know why. Some ghost has locked onto you — you and no one else. And you're telling me that time has no link to it!"

Max noticed Cassie's face pale a bit. He suddenly had a sinking feeling that Caroline might be intent on dredging up some dark family secret that may or may not be relevant. Cassie glared at her daughter with tremendous upset, concern, and what Max detected as a bit of betrayal on her face. "Mom, look, you might need to get this out on the table," Jared piped in. "This ghost woman is targeting you."

Peter was beside Cassie now, his hand on her shoulder. "Look, whatever it is, we don't need to discuss it like this."

Cassie shook her head, her face becoming a bit sterner. "No, no, please, my children want to bring this out! I went through a period of severe depression about a year after Allen died. The stress, revelations about my late husband, all of it came crashing down on me. I saw a therapist, was on medication for a while, and then got off it."

"Aunt Elise had to stay with us because you weren't functioning at all," Caroline whispered.

A few stray tears began to fall from Cassie's eyes, and Max looked down. He felt like he shouldn't be witnessing this. It was too personal. He had no idea why Caroline felt compelled to drag this out so publicly. "Yes, that's true," Cassie said softly. "I'm ashamed of it. I'm ashamed I was so weak then, but I didn't try to kill myself if that's where you're going with this." She directed a bit harshly at her daughter.

"No," she murmured, "you just gave up on yourself and us."

Max couldn't help himself. He grabbed Caroline's shoulders and was shocked at the nearly burning negative energy that he felt on Caroline's skin. Just touching it made him nauseous. "You went somewhere earlier, right after we arrived at the hotel," he said sternly. Caroline looked dazed as though she wasn't hearing him. "Cara!" he repeated a bit more loudly. Her eyes finally focused on him, eyes filled with upset.

"What did you say?" she asked.

"Earlier, when we arrived with Jared, you said you'd meet us upstairs. I took the luggage. Where did you go?"

"Um," she seemed almost completely vague. "The gift shop downstairs. I'd forgotten toothpaste."

His eyes narrowed a bit. "First thing is you need a shower, and Peter and I are going downstairs to check out that gift shop."

And of course, Jared wanted to come with them, but Max managed to convince him to stay in the room with his mother and sister in case of any problems. It was more than clear to him that Caroline's brother had a well-concealed chivalrous vein that made him quite protective over the female members of his family.

"So, do you really think you'll find some great menace in the Hotel Mandolin's gift shop?" They were in the elevator descending to the lobby when Peter hit him with that dry remark.

Max looked at him without expression, asking flatly, "So what is going on with you and Cassie? You seem to have taken on the role of her protector and defender."

In return, Peter eyed him with that cool penetrating stare that Max was more that sure sent chills down the spine of certain unsavory characters. But as it was, it had no effect on him." We've become friends," he said with no further elaboration.

"So, I see," he murmured just as the elevator doors opened.

Cold Spots

Twelve

Max had no idea what he was looking for. All he was doing was feeling. So, without a plan, he crossed the threshold of *The Hotel Mandolin Gift Spot* with no preconceived notions in mind but with his psychic radar turned on full blast.

It was cold. That was the first thing that hit him as he walked inside the rather cozy space of the finely decorated retail shop. The woman behind the counter, possibly in her sixties or early seventies, he surmised, finely groomed, dark hair poofed out, make-up heavily applied, greeted them smoothly. "Are you gentlemen looking for anything in particular?" she asked with a smile heavily accentuated by a rather dark shade of burgundy-colored lipstick. Max could have sworn he'd seen her before, but perhaps again, it was this type of female from a previous generation that he'd seen milling about the shops of Uptown New Orleans.

"Just browsing," he replied with a smile, noting that Peter responded to his response with just a raised eyebrow. As he ignored the lady and Peter for the moment, now focusing on the task at hand, Max allowed himself to sink into a deeper awareness.

He breathed deeply and almost instantly began to see color — manifestations of energy flood the store. His skin began to feel warmth and then heat in specific areas as he slowly walked through the two or three aisles that encompassed the space.

And then, he abruptly stopped his progression. Not because he wanted to but more so because he had no choice. It was somewhere around the middle of the store, something that felt distinctly like a wall, an impediment he'd physically impacted.

The air was heavier, heavy, and icy, but with effort, he forced himself through to the center of the phenomena. Its shape was like a massive cylinder — perhaps a yard or two across, shooting straight up to the ceiling. Max's eyes were watering. The sensation was so dense, and the colors were now blindingly imperceptible. But tangibly, he could feel the negative energy at its center swirling around him like vines, clinging, biting, and stinging parasites. He tried not to breathe too deeply for fear of ingesting something. It was so strong, perhaps plunging straight through the ceiling.

Unable to tolerate it anymore, he stepped backward, nearly colliding with Peter, who managed to step away quickly enough to get out of his way. "Find anything?" he asked with surprise in his voice.

Max's eyes shot to the woman behind the old fashion looking register whose wide dark eyes had not left them. "No," Max said with no emotion, then abruptly headed out of the store.

"Cold spots?"

Max shrugged uncomfortably. They'd returned to Cassie's room, where Caroline had emerged from the shower about as red as a beet. Evidently, she'd taken some time drowning away the residue of her visit to the gift shop. "For lack of a better term."

"That's not unusual with hauntings," Cassie commented.

"Yes," Max said. "But what I experienced was very concentrated."

"Concentrated what?" Peter asked.

"Negative energy, it was concentrated and potent."

Caroline frowned, her hair still dripping. Sitting on the edge of the bed, she murmured, "I don't know why I didn't pick up on it."

"I don't think it's obvious. It seems more insidious. I had to focus very intently at first to pick up on it. But it is particularly toxic," he said, feeling the irritability of the energy clinging to him.

"You might need a shower, too," Caroline said, looking at him more like the woman he adored.

"All of us might need showers," he said grimly. "Clearly, there is more here than meets the eye."

Her head throbbed unmercifully, and she would have liked to go to the hotel gift shop for some aspirin. Unfortunately, that was out of the question now. All this was taking its toll on her — from the vision to the confrontation with her family to Max's revelation about the cold spot downstairs in the gift shop, apparently strong enough to send Caroline a bit over the edge. Cassie stared out the window of her room into the night without really seeing. That was the thrust of it, Caroline bringing out all her dirty laundry for everyone to see. She knew that Caroline hadn't been herself, and had lost control because of the impact of the negative energy. But the truth was that this didn't eliminate the element of choice. For it to be brought out at all, there had to be a seed of discontent.

Caroline walked back into the room. Cassie gathered that she'd been out in the hall talking to Max. She looked different, clearly calmer now. "Max was wondering if we should all go out to dinner somewhere away from here for a little while, just to clear our heads."

"Your brother is still in the shower," Cassie said a little stonily.

"I meant after he gets out."

Cassie stared at her, wondering if she could even comprehend how devastating her words had been. "I don't know," she whispered, walking away and turning her back to her.

Then she felt the very light touch of Caroline's hand on her shoulder. "I'm so sorry, Mom. I shouldn't have done that to you."

She breathed deeply, painfully, from all the emotion lodged in her chest. "Sounded as though you'd been saving it up for a long time," she murmured.

Caroline walked around to face her. "Maybe because I was so young. I didn't understand what was happening. Dad was gone, and you were slipping away too. I was terrified."

"I know. I have a lot of guilt about that. I dropped the ball when you needed me. But as you grow older, maybe you'll understand. We're all human. We all fail sometimes, do things we wish we hadn't, and make choices we regret. And we hope the people we love forgive us. Sometimes they do, and sometimes they don't. Life isn't about perfection. It's about— "

"Learning," Caroline finished.

"Yes," she said, smiling through tears.

"But Mom," she said quietly. "There still is a problem here. Why is Margaret Monjure connecting to you? Don't let her exploit your vulnerabilities."

And at that moment, Cassie felt a tangible chill of concern creep around her heart.

It did help. They'd left the Hotel Mandolin at about seven thirty and headed out to a lovely restaurant on Canal St. called Mandina's. It almost resembled a large cozy house with its massive brick fireplace and high ceiling overhead. Of course, the main dining room was only about six times the size of a typical family den. But it felt oddly comforting. All of them crowded around a great big round table in the corner of the restaurant, laughing and talking. Even Peter seemed quite relaxed within the chaotic bunch. And for a moment, just a moment, Cassie let go and allowed herself to worry about virtually nothing.

"So, we're all squeaky clean. What's the next step in this great adventure?" Jared quizzed.

Max glanced around them at Jared's query. The restaurant was fairly busy, with lots of different conversations going on at the surrounding tables. "Well," he began slowly, "I've been thinking about that. I think we might have to make a trip."

Caroline looked at him with confusion, with her shrimp po'boy in one hand and a large, frosty schooner of beer in the other that she'd stopped sipping at his pronouncement. "A trip now? I thought we had to figure—oh." Max had stopped her in midsentence with a somewhat meaningful look that made Cassie want to giggle.

Peter was frowning, obviously not comfortable being out of the loop. "Trip?" he asked with bewilderment.

"Not an ordinary trip, a psychic one," Max finished in rather hushed tones.

Peter glanced over at Cassie for clarification. She leaned closer to him, which wasn't difficult since he was already in the chair beside hers. "He's talking about a sort of psychic exploration using an out-of-body experience," she whispered.

"Oh, of course," Peter said, with just a hint of sarcasm.

"I think with all of us together. It will give stability to the endeavor. Of course, some will travel, and others will have to stay behind to anchor," Max explained.

"I'm going," Cassie said flatly.

"Mom, I don't know if that's a good idea," Caroline said with concern.

"I'm the one who has gained more information on this than anyone else. You need me to—"

"I agree," Max said flatly. Cassie looked over at him, a bit surprised. "We need Cassie if we're going to get to the bottom of this. Caroline, Cassie, and I will go. Jared and Peter, you will anchor us."

"That sounds like so much fun," Jared said sourly.

Max spoke to him directly. "Look, Jared, I'm depending on you and Peter. We need a strong connection to ground us in this. You possess a lot of untapped power. We need you for this."

Cassie could see Jared's expression change a bit. What Max had said was true. Jared had tremendous psychic potential that was largely unexplored. "All right," he said. "I'll do whatever is needed."

Cassie smiled at him. She was so very proud of both her children. But when she glanced at Peter, she noticed that he had a strange look. There were so many contained emotions that she had no clue what he was feeling.

Traveling

Thirteen

"I'm not convinced this is a good idea," Peter said.

He'd asked Cassie to walk with him for a few moments just after they arrived at the hotel. The two of them had meandered through the main lobby. They'd settled in a cluster of antique-looking, golden wing-backed chairs facing the hotel's famous bronze statue of the wood nymph holding the mandolin nearly at the center of the great room.

Cassie looked at him a bit surprised, but then again, she'd noted he was cautious in some ways. This she'd discovered already over their short acquaintance. "In what respect?" she asked, glancing at a huge brass, ornate clock hung high over the check-in desks. It was already quarter 'til nine. It had been a long day, and it wasn't over yet.

His eyes narrowed a bit. "In all respects."

She frowned with concern, "Really?"

"You, all of you, don't know what you're getting into."

"That's why we're doing this to collect information."

He was looking at her sternly, almost with frustration. "Look, Cassie, to be frank. You're too trusting."

His comment hit her oddly, making her want to smile a bit. "I am?"

"Yes, you need to be more suspicious. It's been my experience that people always have an angle, an agenda.

This whole business, it isn't adding up to me. Something's off here."

"Yes, well, I'd agree with that."

Peter sighed with a touch of frustration. "I'm not articulating this well. If you are determined to do this, you must be alert, defensive, guarded, and protective of yourself. And above all, pull the plug just as soon as you get that feeling."

"That feeling that something is rotten in Denmark?"

He smiled a bit at the reference, "You aren't taking this seriously."

"I am. I trust your instincts, Peter. I promise I will be on my guard in the best tradition of detective fiction."

"One more thing," he said coolly.

"What's that?" she said.

"This," he leaned in and then softly touched his lips to hers.

She couldn't say she didn't expect it. But maybe she didn't expect to like it so much. But when he ended the rather chaste kiss, she couldn't help but wonder what a not-so-chaste one might be like.

Max was taking the lead, and it made sense, she supposed. They had cleared space in Cassie and Caroline's hotel room, moving chairs and shifting the beds just a bit. Max and Caroline had lit white candles that they'd brought with them. Evidently, they had discussed, unbeknownst to her, that attempting this might be a possibility.

All of them, all five of them, sat on the floor in a circle, holding hands. It reminded her of the séances Cassie and Elise would conduct on the back-screen porch of their house on Pritchard Street when they were teenagers. The parallels did strike a chord. After all, they were attempting to contact the dead.

Cassie had taken off her shoes and was sitting on the floor cross-legged. Years of yoga, which she had fallen off of recently, had kept her a bit pliable in such situations. Jared was sitting on one side of her and Peter on the other with Max and Caroline across the circle.

"Everyone, try to get as comfortable as possible," Max calmly directed.

"The grounding portion of this team, what can we expect?" Peter asked. Cassie sensed a bit of gruffness in his tone, which told her he wasn't particularly comfortable mentally or physically.

"You and Jared may see some color variation but nothing much beyond that. The key for you two is not to break the circle so that it will be easier for the rest of us to return."

"And where exactly are you going again?" Peter asked.

"To another plane of reality, where hopefully we can get some answers about what is happening here. Now, Caroline and Cassie, it is essential that the three of us stay together."

"All right," Cassie said. She felt Peter squeeze her hand a bit, and Jared had straightened up his usually slouched frame beside her, seeming to be focusing intently. She was a bit surprised that he was taking all of this so seriously. It was his manner these days to be flip about everything.

"Now, everyone, close your eyes and focus on clearing your mind," Max directed.

Cassie closed her eyes and concentrated on breathing deeply, letting all other earthly concerns melt away. She could feel a power within the circle they'd created, such strong energies emitted by everyone — even from Peter, who she suspected had much stronger psychic abilities than he acknowledged.

These were her thoughts before things began to shift.

Colors, brilliant colors, began to manifest. There was movement within her limbs, even though her body was perfectly still. She breathed in deeply again, feeling a sweep of dizziness overtake her.

And just before she left, she heard Caroline calling from a distance, "Mom, wait."

Cassie felt as though she was opening her eyes, but then she remembered that this wasn't actual vision. Her spirit was traveling. She hesitantly glanced around, knowing clearly that she was not still in the room with everyone.

Concentrating on steadying herself, she allowed her vision to focus slowly. It was a room, a room of the hotel, but clearly different. The furniture around her was more elaborate, with an antiquated style. The sofa where she sat was stiff, more formal, less comfortable. The drapes across the room on a window were long and ornate. There was a fireplace with a dark mahogany mantle, a coffee table with a marble top, and several huge golden gilded mirrors hanging on the wall. She stood up, and again dizziness swirled around her. And in the same moment, it hit her profoundly, accompanied by a definitive chill. She was alone. Max and Caroline weren't with her. She cleared her mind and attempted to focus on their essence, but it was useless. She couldn't reach out here. It felt absolutely muffled.

Glancing around again, she realized she must be in one of the hotel's suites. There seemed to be several adjoining doors to this main room. And then she saw that one of the connecting doors was wide open. Deep down, somewhere, a panic had begun rising within her, but it was buried beneath this sluggish feeling throughout her limbs, enveloping her. She knew she needed to leave and find a way to locate Caroline and Max. But something else drew her to that door, the open one — something strong, compelling her to go inside.

Somewhat reluctantly, she began to move toward it slowly. It felt so much like the sensation of walking, so strange that although she was in some sort of astral state, everything here did feel particularly physical. A coldness swept across her as she paused at the entrance, but it didn't stop her, didn't stop her from pushing forward and peering inside.

Just within, she saw a four-poster, dark wooded bed, and a tall dresser. Across from it was a vanity table made of warm cherry wood with three large connected mirrors on the top.

Cassie stood frozen in the doorway, unable to make herself move. It was oddly mesmerizing because, in front of the mirrors, someone was sitting there — a woman, her back to Cassie. Her dark hair was swept up in a massive poof, like an old-fashioned style they used to call the Gibson girl. And Cassie couldn't help but recognize the dress she wore, that vibrant, midnight blue velvet dress that she'd seen in so many visions. She leaned against the door, feeling petrified and weak, too drained for motion. And then, the woman stood up and turned around slowly.

Cassie swallowed on what felt like a throat dry with fear.

The woman's skin was pale, white, bloodless, clearly the color of a corpse that had been so for some time. And her neck, her neck bore the ugly reddish swollen welts of strangulation. But even more disturbing than all of this were the eyes, the eyes that seemed as lifeless as one after death but which clearly focused on her.

And odd smile lit up the eerily blanched face. "I've been waiting for you," she said in a soft melodious voice.

Cassie could feel the cold emitting from the woman's body even at their distance.

"Margaret, Margaret Monjure," she whispered, choking back on the terror she couldn't help but feel. "What do you want?"

"I want you to stay with me. This is where you belong."

The Tunnels

Fourteen

Caroline felt the transition. It was jarring, not smooth, as she had experienced in the past. It was a rough, jagged jolt that made her feel like her astral self had been ripped from her body.

And then the cold, unbearably cold, a sensation wrapping all around her, nearly suffocating. "Max," she directed outward.

In the next instant, she felt, not so rough, but with more than a bit of determination, being pulled away from wherever she'd landed. "Max," she called out again, unable to clearly sense his presence.

"It's all right," she felt his answer in her mind. And she felt the chill begin to dissipate, and with its retreat, the panic she'd initially experienced began to calm.

Around her, she could see familiar walls around her, those shiny gray walls, the tunnels they'd traveled in with Rick Lightner. "What's happening?"

"Just take a minute," he said. The image of him was beside her now. Things were clearing a bit.

"It's better now," she whispered. "But a moment ago, I felt like I couldn't breathe."

"It was another cold spot, like the one in the gift shop," Max said. "I'm beginning to suspect this place is filled with them, pockets of intensely negative energy."

"What causes them?"

"It's hard to say. They feel very old, maybe the land, things that happened here. I don't know. But that isn't our biggest problem."

Caroline was finally beginning to be able to think more clearly, but then the realization hit her like a sledgehammer. "Oh God, where's Mom?"

"I don't know," Max said grimly. "I can't sense her anywhere."

Cassie dug in. It was a technique that she'd learned a long time ago. It was the thing that got her through the difficult years of her marriage, the thing that pulled her out of her depression when she felt as though everything was collapsing around her. She dug in deep, deep inside herself, to that core of steel, and made herself deal with the horror standing before her.

"No, Margaret, you're wrong. I don't belong here."

The apparition whose flat dark eyes were fixed on her looked confused. "I could feel you, unhappy like me. It's safe here. You and I are the same."

"No, Margaret," she repeated. Again, Cassie steeled herself as that thing moved closer to her. She could smell a horrible stench of decaying flesh emanating from her. She tried to focus — ghosts, trapped spirits, confused, still attached to the flesh although they weren't of the flesh, unable to let go, completely caught up in their torment. "You can't be happy here like this."

Again, the dark eyes seemed hungrily gobbling up this contact with her. "Happy?"

Cassie swallowed, trying desperately not to gag. "I don't understand why you're punishing yourself here, Margaret. It wasn't your fault what happened with your husband."

She tilted her head a bit as though Cassie's words were nonsense. It was sad in a way. She reminded her in some respects of a lost child. "Henri?"

Cassie nodded, "Yes, Henri, he did that to you." She pointed to the red welts on Margaret's waxen flesh.

In response, the woman's hand went to the wounds at her neck, lightly brushing them with her fingertips.

"Yes, he did this. He hated me, said he wanted his freedom."

"That wasn't your fault," Cassie said, desperately trying to reach through the cloud of insanity. "You shouldn't be trapped here. You should go on to somewhere where you can find peace."

Margaret continued staring at Cassie intently as though trying to comprehend. "He did this," she said softly. "Then I pushed him. I pushed him down into that blackness and shattered him."

Cassie's eyes widened. Just as Margaret described what happened, Cassie could see it before her. Margaret had died but used her rage from the beyond to lash out at her killer, filling him with terror and causing him to spill over the railway of the stairs.

With this vision, Cassie felt undeniably as though all the breath and energy had been knocked out of her. These heinous acts had caused both spirits to be launched into their fugue of insanity and trapped here, relentlessly punishing themselves as Margaret's current decrepit state testified to. Trembling all over, Cassie felt blanketed in those emotions of depression, sadness, and confusion that emanated from this tortured ghost. "So, you see," Margaret whispered with her foul breath. "You need to stay with me." And it suddenly flashed across Cassie's mind like a revelation — Janie Tyler. She'd whispered the same to Janie Tyler, but not understanding the calamity she was facing, the girl had crumbled beneath the weight of the toxic emotions.

It felt dark, clammy within the tunnels of the Hotel Mandolin and completely muffled, not to mention claustrophobic. "Why does it seem so horrible here?"

They were cautiously moving through the passage where she and Max had landed not so long ago. "It's the plateau we've landed on."

He continued to move deep in concentration, and she beside him. "But it wasn't like this. I mean, so horrible the last time we were here."

"This isn't reality," he mumbled. "But it is a plane of existence. Try to focus on Cassie. We must find her."

Caroline attempted to clear her mind for the hundredth time, anchoring herself to a vision of her mother. But it was transient, easily clouding over. As they moved on, she continued to hear strange sounds, creaking, shuffling, things dragging in the shadows that seemed to be increasing. "Do you hear that?" she whispered.

"Yes, try to concentrate," he said softly. "You have the strongest link with Cassie."

"What are you doing?" she asked, a bit perturbed.

"Trying to avoid us plunging into another one of those cold spots. We can't afford to lose that much energy again."

On her body, Caroline was feeling things picking at her skin like tiny insects. But in determination, she tried again to connect to Cassie. She could almost see her. She was in a room somewhere, but then it was muffled out like something snuffing out the light of a candle. "I don't think she's here, not in the tunnels."

"Neither do I," Max grumbled. She could hear the irritation in his voice as well. And lucky for her, she was empathic enough to know that it had nothing to do with her. This place, this plane as he called it, was gnawing at him as well.

"Well, how—" Then she stopped. She'd caught sight of something in the periphery of her vision, a movement in the shadows.

Max grabbed her hand, or rather Max's astral self, which felt strangely corporeal just now. "Quiet," he murmured quickly.

They watched in silence as the shadows moved, tentatively at first, then separating, forming. Caroline felt completely stunned when after the longest interval, it finely took shape — because it was a person, a tall dark-haired man dressed in a suit. But the figure was still predominantly hidden in the shadows. "Just be calm," Max whispered. She couldn't make out the man's face, just his form, but clearly, he was slowly heading in their direction. "Remember, this isn't reality, Cara," he said carefully, "just someone's perception of it."

His movement was uneven, a sort of dragging motion toward them. And then, a calm, cultured voice came out of the darkness. "I'm sorry. I was wondering if you might help me. I seem to have lost my way."

Caroline almost responded, but again Max grabbed her arm to restrain her. The tall figure continued to shuffle toward them. His suit was different somehow, she thought, the cut antiquated, not at all current. But with a few more steps, the dim light finally hit him so that she could make out his features.

It was impossible, jarring, that mixture of horror and nausea. His skin was white, pure white, as though all the blood had drained from it. Just on the side of his head, black scorching, torn, decaying flesh, where it was clear a projectile, possibly a bullet, had passed into his head. "Remember, this isn't real."

"What?" she gasped.

"It's how he perceives himself."

Caroline was breathing deeply, trying to piece it together. "I don't—who is he?"

"I'm Gerald," he said a bit hesitantly. "I've lost my way," he reiterated, sounding fearful and confused.

"He's one of our suicides," Max said quietly.

"What happened to Janie Tyler?" she asked. Cassie's head was spinning with dizziness, and the woman, although she'd rather say the creature, was so close to her that she felt like gagging.

"The little girl," it said.

"Yes, I can feel her near you."

The mouth on her arched ever so slightly in a smile, and Cassie wondered for the first time if Margaret Monjure had become evil somehow. It wasn't unheard of that when one obtained power, any kind of power, it could corrupt you, even in this distorted nightmarish realm. "She was sad," she rasped.

"Like you?" Cassie asked.

"No," she shook her head, noting that the pinned-up coiffure was falling in places. The once lush brunette hair was brittle and shriveling like all the rest of her. "She was weak. Weak in life, letting everything overpower her, diminish her. So, she's here now where I keep her safe." Cassie glanced around the room. It was empty, except for the two of them. "Not here," she said, her flat eyes showing no animation as if they'd been constructed of plastic.

"Where is she?" Cassie asked.

"Hiding, they're all hiding."

Gerald

Fifteen

"Gerald, how did you get here?" Max asked as calmly as if he were talking to a waiter in a restaurant. The man, rather the corpse-like man, as Caroline had come to categorize him in her mind, glanced around almost fearfully. "It's all right. You can talk to us," Max said soothingly.

"I came here from my office."

"Your office in the city?"

He nodded slowly. "Yes, just for a night, I thought to clear my head. I couldn't go home, not the way things were. You see, I'd lost everything. Everyone did. The banks had no money, and I couldn't go home. So, I came here, just for a while."

"The crash," Max murmured.

"You mean the Stock Market Crash?" Caroline nearly exploded.

"But you didn't leave?"

"I, I don't know. I got lost here, after—" he hesitated. "And there was the woman, the woman in the blue dress. She told me to rest and that it was safe here, but in a little while, she would help me. Help me go home."

"No concept of time," Max whispered.

Caroline's heart clutched painfully in her chest. She was picking up his emotions now, so much fear, confusion, despair. He didn't remember shooting himself, just being lost and trapped. So much worse than the life he was trying to escape.

Max squeezed her hand. "You have to guard against connecting with them too much. It will overwhelm you."

She nodded, trying to mentally erect a wall around her, preventing her empathic psychic abilities from linking with the lost soul in front of her.

"Are there others?" Max asked.

And Gerald looked at him with almost amazement, "Yes, many."

Peter opened his eyes. He'd been focusing, finding himself wrapped in what he could only describe as a blanket of white light that was peaceful and calming. He'd been content to stay there until he felt it — like a cold splash of ice water dropping down on him, sending a wild alarm of concern crashing across his mind.

Around him, everyone was still there but motionless, seemingly deep inside the meditation. But suddenly, Jared Breslin's dark blue eyes snapped open as well. And immediately, he said, "What is it?" his youthful voice laced with the alarm that Peter was feeling.

"I don't know. I just have a bad feeling something is wrong and that your Mom is in trouble."

He could tell by the expression on Jared's face that this was not far afield from what the young man was feeling. "I know. I could see her, but she was not with the others. She was with something else."

"How can we get to her?" Peter snapped out, not entirely knowing what he was asking.

Jared's face steeled in determination in a way that seemed well beyond his years. "We can try something."

"Let's do it," then he rethought it. "What exactly?"

"I'm going to focus on sending you to Mom."

"What? I mean, is that possible?"

"We're going to find out."

"You know. I'm not a psychic like you guys, kiddo."

"Well, like Aunt Elise says, everyone is a psychic. Are you willing?" he asked with undeniable determination in his young voice.

"Yes," he responded, having no clue what he might be getting himself into. "But what do I do if I get there?"

"Bring her back." Peter hesitated, then nodded. "Now close your eyes and concentrate on Mom, being with her."

"Okay," Peter said, settling in again. "Are you sure you can handle things here?"

"Don't worry about me," was the last thing he heard Jared say before things began to escalate.

Caroline felt light-headed, but Max wrapped his arm around her, pulling her tightly against his side as they walked. Then again, she had to remind herself that they weren't in physical form. It was confusing. They'd traveled before. The two of them, in this way, traveled with no one behind anchoring them. And at times, it felt very disconnected, as though there were no bodies. And at other times, like this one, she did feel distinctly physical. Max had explained that it depended on the specific plane you were exploring. This one appeared to be largely a manifestation of others' reality. A place between, he called it. Not their world and not the next, so whoever was stuck here sort of filled it in with their interpretation of things.

"It's so dark," she murmured.

"Yes, true," Max responded. He seemed hesitant to say much as they followed closely behind their new guide through the slimy, dank tunnels. Gerald, who she gleaned had shot himself sometime around the Stock Market Crash at the end of the twenties, was their new best friend, at least for the present in this convoluted reality.

"Where are we going again?" Caroline whispered.

"I believe to the others he referred to."

"You think Mom is with them?"

"We can hope," he replied, holding her close as they made their slow progress behind Gerald.

Their ghost guide suddenly stopped, then began an ascent up a short metal staircase to a door he, without hesitation, pulled open. Rather quickly, he walked, or should she rather say shuffled inside. He had disappeared into the darkened opening, but Caroline hesitated, feeling a tangible iciness rush out from that direction. "Max!"

"I know," he interrupted. "But we have to go forward if we want to find Cassie. I'll go first," he said. Caroline nodded but continued to hold onto the back of his shirt as they moved forward.

Peter felt sick — dizzy, disoriented, and more than a bit nauseous. He simply allowed himself to sink down to the cold floor as he tried to catch his breath. Vision was spotty, so he opted to close his eyes for a moment trying to regroup. "Focus, focus on Mom," he heard a distant voice, although it didn't seem all that distant because it was coming from inside his head.

"Jared," he whispered, still trying to quell the extreme turbulence in his stomach.

"Mr. Norfleet, I'm trying to guide you. You must clear your mind and focus on where you are."

"Peter, please, kiddo." He raised his head and forced his eyes to open, although, on some level, he would have much preferred to curl up into a ball and go to sleep — so many divergent reactions he was dealing with. As he continued to look around, his vision seemed to steady a bit, enough for him to recognize somewhat where he was. "This looks to be the lobby."

"Is Mom there?"

Rubbing his eyes a bit more, he tried again to canvas his surroundings. "I don't see anybody. It's empty."

"Peter," the distant voice.

"Yeah, kid."

"You might need to look for her."

"Yeah, but that would entail getting up."

"Take it slow."

"There's no other way I can take it," he grimaced. Shakily and at a snail's pace, he got to his feet, deliberately ignoring the dizziness. He really didn't get it. He thought the point of astral travel was to leave behind the physical body. But he felt every little ache and pain he had supposedly left back in Cassie's hotel room. Straightening up again, he looked around. Same lobby, he remembered, although definitely a bit colder, a bit arctic, in fact. He began to walk, still painfully slow, past the empty front desk, down the short spray of golden steps, and stopping right in front of the lounge housed inside the hotel — The Cavern. He remembered it from the hotel literature, opening in the early 1900s under the same name. He had thought about taking Cassie there for a late-night drink, but that was before all these supernatural traveling plans were made.

Peter started to walk past it, continuing to explore the rest of the lobby, but something made him stop again. "Go see," Jared's voice.

"You still here?"

"As long as I can be. It's tough. This is draining. It would be better if you moved quickly."

"Right, I'll work on that," he grumbled, now heading into The Cavern with a purpose. It was actually a larger space than one might expect from the outside. It was filled with actual cave like décor — plaster stalactites on the ceiling, stalagmites coming off the bar, cave-like murals painted on the walls, and all of it colored in grays, pink, and blues a bit like, well, clearly someone's interpretation of a cave. He glanced around, seeing what he'd expected. Basically, it was an empty club, and then he paused for a moment. He'd almost missed it. But deep in the corner, at a small round table, someone was there, sitting, watching him, as still as a mouse.

His heart did a bit of a flip of surprise at the sight. It wasn't Cassie, but it was someone else that he did recognize. He walked toward the figure, feeling the already chilling temperature perceptively dip the closer he got.

She looked up at him with very wide brown and particularly fearful eyes. "You can see me," she whispered.

He nodded, slowly sitting on the cold, slate-gray colored chair across from her. "Talk to her. It's okay," Jared prodded. Pushy kid, he thought.

"Are you all right?" he said.

She tilted her head just a fraction at him, the eyes seeming just a notch less fearful. "I think I'm dead. Is that true?" she asked.

Talk about starting with a blunt question. But then again, that was often his technique. Peter didn't know what the protocol was in this kind of situation. But on the whole, he'd always thought if someone asked an honest question that, it might be best to give them a truthful answer. "Yes, Janie, I'm afraid you are."

She frowned. "You know my name."

"Yeah, actually, I've been working for your parents."

Janie Tyler

Sixteen

The doorway opened into a long hallway, not unlike the one that led to their hotel rooms on the fifth floor. Gerald continued to shuffle forward, but then Max called out to him. "Gerald, we need to know exactly where you are taking us."

The man stopped and turned around, facing them with confusion on his pale, gaunt face. But then again, admittedly, Caroline had noticed that expression more than once since they'd met him. "You wanted to see the others."

"Actually, we're looking for someone else Gerald, someone like us that might be lost here."

"Lost here?" he repeated.

"Yes, my mother," Caroline said. "We got separated. She was looking for a woman here, a woman in a blue dress named Margaret Monjure."

"That woman," Gerald repeated, but Caroline saw something had changed. There was a distinct shaking fear in his voice now. "No, I can't take you there."

Max stepped back a bit, and then Caroline saw why. There were people behind him now, behind Gerald that hadn't been there a moment before. There was an old man; another woman at his side, younger, more modern, but with wounds on her, gunshot wounds; and then another man pushing his way forward, the frame of his body distinctively broken as though he'd had a fall. And there were others, so many of them, all damaged to different degrees.

"Oh God," she whispered, trying to quell her instinctive horror at their appearance.

"Try to keep calm," Max told her, his voice steady.

"More suicides?" she murmured.

"Most likely."

"We need to find this woman," Max said calmly but with steel in his voice.

And then that man, the mangled one, worked his way to the front of the group. As he moved, Caroline had the profound sensation that his body was broken in places. It was so strong, emanating from him, the pain in his arm, his spine, and his shoulders that were hunched up in an abnormal fashion. "Margaret you want," he rasped. It was a terrible feeling coming from him, rage, pure rage but also fear that Caroline felt.

"Don't connect with them," Max warned her. "There is too much unstable emotion here, disproportionate pain and unstable emotion."

Caroline stepped back a few spaces, willing a shield of white light around her again.

Max turned to address the man who now stood in front of the small group of unfortunate souls. "I know who you are."

"Do you? And you still seek that woman?"

"We have to find her. I'm sure she knows where Cassie is."

He looked at Max oddly and then focused directly on Caroline with his black eyes. "If she has your mother, my dear, she's already lost."

At first, he hadn't realized it, but Janie Tyler was dressed in night clothes. She wore a long-oversized t-shirt that said Loyola Rocks and a pair of sweatpants. At least, that seemed the equivalent of night clothes for America's modern youth. And she also looked pale, sickly pale, with great big dark splotches under her eyes, indicating that she hadn't rested for some time.

She had a pen and a small notebook in front of her. Evidently, she'd been writing something when he'd interrupted her. "I didn't intend to die," she said flatly.

"But the pills, you overdosed."

She nodded, her eyes narrowing a bit. "You know, I thought about it a long time after I got here. I was confused, and there was that woman. Have you seen her?"

He frowned, suddenly realizing she'd assumed he was dead just like her. "Woman? No, I actually came here looking for someone in particular."

"Well, that woman, the one in the long blue dress, gets her hands on everyone as soon as they come here." She leaned in toward him, her pale pixyish face looking a bit conspiratorial. "It's like she owns the place. And everyone's afraid of her. It's so strange." Then she frowned, "You're not going to tell her that I said that are you?"

"No, of course not, but you said you weren't trying to die."

"No, I mean I was feeling sad and depressed. This place does that to you. I mean, like it makes you feel so tired and then so sad. But I got confused. I didn't remember taking the pills, the ones to help me sleep. It was like I forgot."

"That shouldn't have caused your death."

Then she looked up at him wide-eyed in a way that reminded him very much of his daughter Jessie. "But I think it happened more than once."

"More than once you forgot? How many times, Janie?"

"Four or five I think," then she frowned again repeating. "This place, it makes you forget."

She needed to get away. That was the one coherent thought that Cassie seemed able to hang onto. "You can't leave here," Margaret whispered harshly.

"I'm not like you," she said, pushing hard to get the words out.

"You're wrong. That's why I brought you here. You're just like me, so sad, so lost. I had children too, children back at home, but Henri didn't think about them, only thought about what he wanted."

"Where is he? Henri?" Cassie asked, feeling as though she had to keep her talking until she could find some way out of this.

"Henri? He's around here hiding somewhere. He's always so afraid, dragging that broken body of his around," she said with a hint of a smile that made Cassie's blood freeze.

"But you did that to him."

The corpse-like head tilted a bit as though there weren't many other options available for expression. "He deserved it."

"When you choose revenge, it takes its toll on you."

"What did you expect me to do?"

"Let his karma take care of his accountability," Cassie whispered. "Then his choices wouldn't affect your spirit."

Again, the head tilted, "And I thought I was the one who was mentally damaged."

It was becoming clear that trying to reason with her at this point would be next to impossible. Margaret grinned a bit. "You know. I can feel such strong energy from you Cassandra, not like the others, not so weak. You should stay here with me."

Cassie closed her eyes reaching out, reaching out to anyone who could help.

"Can you take me to where that woman is?"

Janie's already wide eyes managed to widen more. "It's dangerous. She makes you weak, so weak you can't think anymore."

"Energy drainer," Jared interjected.

106

"I thought you'd left."

"Are you talking to someone else?" Janie asked.

Peter grimaced a bit. How to explain all this to the ghost? "Well, sort of. Look, I don't have much time. Will you help me?"

"I thought you were going to help me?"

"I am. I promise, one thing at a time — the woman in the blue dress."

She stood up, leaving the tablet on the table in front of her. "I'll try. But she's dangerous."

"That's okay. I've dealt with dangerous before."

She couldn't remember how many people Peter Norfleet said had committed suicide since the Hotel Mandolin opened in the late 1890s, but the hotel hallway looked pretty full to her. In fact, several dozen people were standing behind Gerald, and the man she had gleaned was Henri Monjure.

"All of these were suicides?" she rasped a bit at Max.

"Suicides, violent, upsetting deaths, people who didn't cross over for some reason." Max's usually calm voice sounded a bit strident and shaky to her. "Henri Monjure," Max directed to the semi-mangled man closest to him. "All of these people are trapped here?"

"Trapped?" he asked. "What else is there?"

Caroline behind him squeezed his hand as Max glanced among the crowd of fearful souls. "There is much more."

"There's a suite up on the seventh floor where she is."

Peter could feel pain in his heart as he ascended the fourth level of stairs. His breathing was becoming a bit heavier. He'd been slacking off at the gym lately, and this was his reward for it. "Why didn't we take the elevators?" he asked.

"They don't always work," Janie said in a rather sprightly manner. The exertion didn't seem to be bothering her at all. Of course, she had died relatively young.

She had led him to a rather obscure stairwell well off the beaten track. It was clear to him that she knew her way around this place backward and forwards. "So, how do you spend your time here?" he asked as she launched up another flight of stairs, her rather large pink slippers flopping hard on the granite.

"Mostly looking for a way out. I don't spend much time with the others. They're so upset and angry at times. I think I'm different," she said, not slowing her quick pace. "I think it's because I didn't mean to kill myself. That has a different effect, at least on how you think about things. I think I just got caught in a bottleneck here."

"A bottleneck?"

"Yeah, so many others were here that I got trapped with them."

"So, you think they belong here?"

"No," she scoffed in her light tone. "I don't think anybody belongs here."

Janie Tyler came off the landing of the stairs and paused in front of a heavy metal door. "This is it," she murmured hesitantly.

She met Peter's gaze with those huge brown eyes. "Are you sure you want to do this?"

"Do you want to stay here?" he asked.

"No," she said without hesitation.

"I think this is the only way out."

"Okay," she said, pulling on the door. "But don't forget, she's dangerous. She's not at all like any of the others." Janie walked down the long hall of a hotel corridor and stopped in front of a long white door whose rather ornate oval metal plate read Suite 703. She backed away from it, looking at Peter. "She's in there."

"Aren't you coming?" he asked.

She shook her head. "I can't. I've been there. I can't again."

He nodded, feeling even more concerned than he had moments ago. "Okay," he said, turning the brass doorknob. He noted for the first time that it was not one of the slide-in computerized keys but a regular, although granted rather ornate, old-fashioned metal doorknob.

"Be careful," Janie said softly. And he remembered cautioning Cassie in the same way just before she had undertaken her journey.

Lost Souls

Seventeen

Cassie could feel it, feel it pressing in on her. Just like the old days when she couldn't think, sometimes couldn't move. Depression can be debilitating, they'd told her. And it was like a cloud around her, a mist she couldn't see through. "Everyone has left you," she could hear Margaret Monjure's voice whispering to her. "But it's safe here. And they can't hurt you anymore."

Cassie was sitting on the floor, leaning against a wall, although she didn't remember getting into that position. She didn't know exactly where Margaret was. Everything seemed like a fog around her, a heavy gray fog filled with that sadness, that oppressive depression she remembered so clearly now.

She tried to focus, focus on clearing her mind, remembering the faces, all the faces of the people she loved — her children, her sister, and there was Max and Peter now, so much to live for. "They're gone. They've left you," she continued to push, and it made Cassie so tired, so completely exhausted just listening to her voice.

"No," she struggled to fight. "You're wrong."

"Cassie," she heard her name being called distantly and heard the reaction of the corpse-like woman — a hiss, nearly like that of a serpent.

When Peter opened the suite door, he felt like he was walking into a freezer. It was even colder than he'd already experienced and much worse because it was pitch black. He took a few steps inward, feeling distinctly as though he couldn't breathe. "What—" he gasped.

"No, this is it."

"I can't see anything," he muttered as he tried to walk deeper into the freezing darkness.

"Try to focus," Jared coaxed. "Focus on seeing."

Peter stood still, directing his eyes on one spot in the darkness, willing with all his energy for his vision to clear. Just slightly, slightly the room began to illuminate, as though, in some respect, he was participating in creating its reality. "Good, keep going," Jared encouraged.

Again, he used his concentration to will more light, and his surroundings responded, beginning to become more visible. It was old, not antique, although there was that. But everything was covered by dust, cobwebs, and mold, and the wallpaper was torn, peeling down in huge strips off the walls. There was dirt, decaying cushions on the sofa, and cracked mirrors on the walls. Everything around him smacked of deterioration. "What the hell lives here?" he asked no one in particular.

"A ghost," Jared answered from somewhere far away. "And from what I gather, an insane one."

And just at that moment, as if on cue, one of the closed doors leading to another room in the suite swung open. Peter couldn't help but gasp a bit. He'd never been much for horror movies, but this definitely felt as though he were now trapped in the genre. Clearly, he'd found her in all her decaying glory—the lady in the blue dress.

"Welcome," she said. A tendril of disgust went up his spine as the corpse-like face smiled.

He steeled himself. Peter wasn't unaccustomed to steeling himself. He had done so in the past many times in the face of evil, or rather, as he preferred to qualify, in the face of those who had chosen to do evil, a bit of a difference. He wasn't a man who really believed in evil in a pure form, but he did believe in choice. Everyone had a choice, and this creature had made some bad ones somewhere along the way.

"Where's Cassie?" he said sternly.

She moved across that threshold rather fluidly for someone who looked like they'd just crawled out of a grave. The infamous blue dress was in tatters, decaying a bit like much of the rest of the room. He certainly didn't need to ask who lived here anymore. It was more than evident.

"She's not here," she rasped, moving that thin gash that barely qualified as a mouth.

"Now we both know that's not true."

The head with its straggly black hair piled high atop it tilted a bit, those cold flat eyes reflecting no expression. "Are you a suitor?" she asked.

The question jolted him, unexpected, to say the least. "I'm a friend."

"That husband of hers nearly destroyed her. She wants no more of your kind."

By his kind, he assumed that she meant men but didn't feel inclined to explore it any further. "You'll excuse me if I don't accept that you have her best interests at heart."

Again, the head tilted as though she were considering him. "I'll let you leave. Go back to your life. But Cassandra will stay with me."

"You must be crazy if you think I'll let her stay with you." And then, of course, he remembered this was the insane ghost that Jared had mentioned.

"You need to convince her to move on. That's what Aunt Elise says. Ghosts are souls trapped between. She needs to move into the light," Jared said a bit frantically.

Move on, okay, new agenda. "So, Margaret, this can't be very nice for you here."

"You can leave, and I will promise not to harm the girl."

"The girl?" he asked.

"The girl who led you to me, I can damage her greatly unless you leave without Cassandra."

"How about we all leave?" Another head tilt. "That's right. I leave with Cassie and you and Janie, and whoever else is here moves on, leaves this place, moves on to another life."

"This is life. This is all there is."

He shook his head, "No, no, it isn't. There is something better out there with people who care about you. Where you're not stuck here with everything," he choked back at all the vivid descriptions that sprang to mind, "with everything falling apart."

"He's right, Margaret," and at that moment, she came out of the open doorway — Cassie, looking exhausted and so pale, but it was her. His heart leaped at the sight of her. He'd been so worried that he would somehow be too late. "What is here is a trap, a terrible place you are trapped in."

Margaret looked at them both, to him, then back to Cassie, as though they were being nonsensical. "You're wrong. This is my place. I am master here, and now no one will leave."

Then behind him from the doorway, Peter heard Max's voice, "No, Margaret, you're wrong. The hallway behind me is filled, filled with lost souls who are ready to go home."

> *Cloudy banks and desperate calls,*
> *Stuck between these horrid walls*
> *Waiting for measure*
> *And lost without hope*
> *Breathless from guarded treasure.*

"Margaret," from a great and distant tunnel. "Time to stop," it says.

She turned her eyes, but the vision was embattled, cloudy. Everyone around her glowed, glowed with a light she'd forgotten.

"We can help you, Margaret," she reached out to draw. To pull that light into her, to strengthen, but her fingers simply passed through. Something had been lost, shifted. "You can move on," the woman with the golden hair said. Emma, her daughter's hair was golden like honey, and she'd run her fingers through it so long ago, just before she'd gone to sleep. The child had smelled like life. It was something that she couldn't smell anymore, not even in memory.

"Margaret, remember," it was Henri's voice before, long before now.

"I can't," she whispered, walking backward, backward into her safe room, backward into the wall, melting away.

Cassie watched the ghost disappear, Margaret Monjure, dissipating as though she didn't exist. Her head throbbed as she felt herself sink to the floor. Then she felt Peter's arm beneath her, supporting her and pulling her to her feet.

"What happened to her?" he asked.

"It was too overwhelming for her. But the others, we need to help them."

Caroline was beside her as well, and the presence of her family around her strengthened Cassie in her terribly depleted state.

"Where's Jared?" she asked.

"He's anchoring all of us and guiding me through this." She smiled at Peter weakly, feeling the pain of the tremendous loss of energy from her heart area.

"I don't think we can stay here much longer," she murmured weakly.

Max nodded, closing his eyes for a moment, then reopening them. "It feels like there is a door opening now. We can try to help those who are willing to cross over."

"Where is it?" Caroline asked.

"I think," Max began focusing intently, "somewhere around the swimming pool."

Caroline looked at him, a bit bemused. "Of course it is."

The Bridge

Eighteen

They gathered out on the deck of the fourth floor. All four of them were holding hands and focusing what energy they had left on the doorway opening just above the covered Olympic-size swimming pool. Cassie focused and then prayed. She did not doubt that a higher power was now leading the charge here, coming to collect and take the lost ones home.

"It's all right now," Max directed to the damaged group of souls that seemed too frightened to embark on this unknown element of a crucial journey. "Your loved ones are waiting for you to guide you," he said. But even their bold friend Gerald looked at him with terror in his eyes.

Then something Cassie hadn't expected happened. Peter broke the group's circle and moved over to a slight figure of a girl that Cassie did not recognize. He held out his hand and waited as the young woman walked tentatively toward him, taking it. "Janie, I promised I would help you. This is the way."

She glanced over to the growing light forming over the pool and a semi-transparent walkway leading toward it. "Are you sure about this?" she said a bit timidly.

"Yeah, I'm sure, kiddo. That's the way out. You've been brave all this time, just a little longer."

She nodded, still looking a bit hesitant. "Just one favor."

Peter smiled, and Cassie could feel his attachment to the girl. "Anything."

"I left my journal back in The Cavern. Will you make sure my parents get it?"

He nodded, "Absolutely."

Then the girl stepped out onto a bridge that seemed invisible but at the same time held her weight as though it were as solid as anything could be. Deliberately, with a confident stride, she moved into that great glowing light without looking back. The next was Gerald, and the others followed more and more quickly behind. Caroline watched them disappear into the light, one by one, painfully aware that this group wasn't as large as the one she'd seen in the hotel corridor. Some, she felt certain, had opted out of the process.

But by the time all had disappeared, one still stood behind, waiting on the pool's edge. And Caroline recognized the mangled body of Henri Monjure. He stood there watching as the last soul disappeared into the light.

Cassie walked up to him, trying to quell her instinctive revulsion at the sight of him. "You can move on as well, Henri," she said softly.

"Can I?" he answered with a rasp. "Aren't I damned eternally?"

She swallowed, feeling Peter's eyes on them and wondering how to answer this. "I can't say that you won't face consequences on the other side Henri. I'm not your judge. You are."

"It's not right that I should leave her alone after what I did."

Cassie sighed, feeling such overwhelming sadness wrapping around her. "That is her choice, you know. You must make yours."

He hesitated a moment longer, looking forward, and then with determination, began to drag himself across the invisible bridge. Once he disappeared into the light, Max, Caroline, and Peter surrounded her. "We need to go, Mom," Caroline said.

But Cassie looked at the flickering light before them with an overwhelming sense of desolation. "I wanted her to move on. She was as lost as any of them."

Then she felt Peter's hand softly touch her shoulder. "As you said, it is her choice."

So tired, so sleepy, it was quiet now. But she remembered her little girl, how she'd run her fingers through her long thick, honey-colored hair.

"Mama," she whispered.

"Emma, my little girl, I'm waiting for everyone to return."

"Come home with me, Mama," her beautiful little girl held out her small hands. "Come home with me." She was so tired, and she was forgetting everything now.

"Mama," she said, holding out her little hands. Margaret took them and felt their warmth, then walked with her little girl into the light.

When Cassie returned to her body, she was trembling. It was so cold, and she was so exhausted. "Jared, Jared," she whispered as she felt Peter helping her to her feet.

"I'm okay, Mom," she nodded, feeling his hug, unable to stop the tears from rolling down her face.

"Everybody is going to need some rest," Max said.

But Cassie was so happy that she couldn't help the tears running down her face. Her children were with her hugging her, and they'd all come home safe.

Cassie, Caroline, and Jared stood in the airport waiting for Elise to depart from her plane. It was a Saturday, and they'd all spent nearly a week following the events at the Mandolin sleeping as much as possible. Max explained that the problem at the Hotel Mandolin wasn't exactly fixed. There were substantial cold spots, or rather concentrations of negative energy, scattered throughout the hotel that had undoubtedly influenced many of the people there who'd taken their own lives. But they had encouraged many of them to cross over, and that had, for lack of a better description, lightened the weight of hauntings at the place. Cassie even felt deep in her heart of hearts, with nothing to back it up, that Margaret Monjure had managed to move on as well. Believing that gave her some peace of mind. Because she'd always believed at the heart of any wrongdoing was a profound sadness.

"Are you seeing Peter again tonight?" Caroline asked.

"No, not tonight. I wanted to spend some time with Elise." Caroline smiled at her with a knowing expression, but Cassie chose to ignore it. Peter had become a bit of a fixture around their house in the weeks since they'd left the Hotel Mandolin. But she couldn't help it. With Jared's aid, he had pretty much launched into the pit of hell to rescue her. And what girl, even one her age, could resist that? And Janie Tyler's journal that he'd retrieved from the lost and found at The Cavern did manage to bring some solace to her parents, which had made his unexpected journey doubly worth it.

As Elise, looking a bit disheveled, made the long walk past the metal detectors toward them, Cassie couldn't help but feel blessed — blessed and more hopeful for the future than she had in some time. As Elise finally reached them with a big smile and a bit of a tan, she threw her arms around Cassie, asking enthusiastically, "Now, what did I miss?"

Finis

More Books by Evelyn Klebert

Gravier's Bookshop
A New Orleans Paranormal Mystery (#1)
6 x 9 Softcover 190 pages
ISBN 978-1-61342-288-5

Caroline Breslin always knew that she would have to live her life differently. Being an extremely sensitive and gifted empath in a family full of psychics has led her to a somewhat cautious existence. But she is determined to strike out on her own, moving out of the protection of her Prytania Street home. And all is going well, except, of course, if you don't count the neighbor upstairs in her apartment building, who may or may not be a dark witch, and the increasing flow of malevolent energy that seems to be directed just her way. All of that and trying to make ends meet seems a bit much for this rather inexperienced New Orleans girl. The last thing Caroline wants to do is run back to her family for help, even though she is painfully in over her head. What she really needs is a knight in shining armor or maybe just that guy that keeps haunting her dreams.

Max Gravier had no intention of becoming a recluse, but after his wife's death, it seems his life is heading in that direction. He spends his time running Gravier's Bookshop on Magazine Street and occasionally, on the quiet, helps the police solve a crime with his psychic sensitivities. That is until he answers Caroline Breslin's call, a cry for help out of his dreams that draws him rather unexpectedly into a fierce battle for a young woman's soul. Join them and the whole Breslin family psychic clan in this first installment of The New Orleans Paranormal Mystery Series, where you'll travel into a

new world just a few steps into the turbulent realm of
the unseen.

The Hotel Mandolin
A New Orleans Paranormal Mystery (#2)
6 x 9 Softcover 138 pages
ISBN 978-1-61342-290-8

Peril is wrapped up in the most enticing of disguises in
The Hotel Mandolin, the second installment of The New
Orleans Paranormal Mystery series. It's opulent, classic,
and one of the most renowned hotels nestled deep in
New Orleans' famous business district, but something is
amiss at The Hotel Mandolin. PI Peter Norfleet is calling
out the big guns to help him investigate a recent suicide
at the famous establishment — his good friend Max
Gravier, a formidable psychic, and his girlfriend,
Caroline Breslin, a talented empath. But none of them
can seem to scratch the surface of this puzzle, no one
except Cassie Breslin, Caroline's clairvoyant mother,
who has somehow tapped into an unexpected
connection with a tragic ghost from the turn of the
century. And the more she uncovers, the more
dangerous and malevolent the mystery becomes.

More Books by Evelyn Klebert

The House at Pritchard Place
A New Orleans Paranormal Mystery (#3)
6 x 9 Softcover 136 pages
ISBN 978-1613422922

Nothing is really wrong with the old Warrick House on Dante St., except that there most certainly is. Nothing is exactly wrong with its new mysterious owner except that Elise is sure something doesn't add up. It isn't obvious, but sometimes the most dangerous things aren't. In the third installment of The New Orleans Paranormal Mystery series, with the help of her very psychic sister and her children, the Breslin clan, Elise Ashford is about to embark on a wild rescue mission straight into another dimension that will land her squarely somewhere she doesn't expect, right back into her past. She'll land full circle; in a childhood home whose memory still haunts her to this day — The House at Pritchard Place.

A Quiet Moment
6 x 9 Softcover 295 pages
ISBN 978-1-61342-326-4

Jacob Wyss is caught in a rut, in fact, on the verge of being engulfed by it. After an excruciating and disillusioning divorce, his life as an artist in a sleepy-college town at the foot of the Appalachian mountains has become quiet, routine, and maddening in its predictability. One wintry day, his deep restlessness drives him out in precarious conditions to a largely empty bookstore nearly devoid of another living soul, nearly.

Aimee Marston isn't like everyone else. On the surface, she lives a sedate life working as a feature writer for a small local newspaper in addition to several other editorial jobs to help make ends meet. But just beneath, her existence is largely not her own. She is a sensitive, an empathic psychic, guided by her calling to use her gifts to help others. Unfortunately, as a result, her secretiveness has made her defensive and protective of herself, preventing her from having much of a life.

A psychic call for help sends Aimee out on a freezing January morning, where her destiny and Jacob's collide, spiraling both their lives onto an unexpected and often disturbing track. Two lonely souls connect, not by accident, but by design. Theirs is the intersection of two spiritual paths, two lovers who must struggle to overcome the phantoms of a past life, as well as the challenges of their own inner demons to carve out an extraordinary future together.

Treading on Borrowed Time
6 x 9 Softcover 198 pages
ISBN 978-1-61342-214-4

For Julia Moreau, life seems complicated. Emerging from a failed marriage and managing a lifetime of diabetes, she lives alone in her childhood home, where she communicates with the spirit of her Great Aunt

More Books by Evelyn Klebert

Lilia. But Julia doesn't have a clue what complicated is until she is thrust into being the key chess piece in a match between two powerful men of extraordinary abilities on the wild hunt for a mystical creature hidden in the heart of New Orleans' French Quarter. Will Julia lose her soul to the karma of a devastating past life or her heart to the love of a man driven by dark forces? What is clear is that whichever way she turns, she is *Treading on Borrowed Time.*

Sanctuary of Echoes
6 x 9 Softcover 338 pages
ISBN 978-1-61342-211-3

Ghosts unacknowledged do not sleep.

Corey Knight has resigned herself to a quiet, reclusive life spent living out the rest of her days in her childhood home on the fringes of New Orleans' French Quarter. But the unexpected specter of her deceased father plunges her into a mad quest for a missing supernatural weapon unearthed long ago. And unfortunately, her only ally is a lost love she once betrayed.

Iain Shaw returns to New Orleans, a city he abandoned a decade before while fleeing a devastating past. Here, he is forced to confront it again in the visage of the woman he once adored - one that he is now determined to get back at any cost.

Follow them both in a wild paranormal tale of discovery and redemption as they confront and unearth the echoes of a buried and unyielding truth that once tore them irreparably apart.

Dragonflies - Journeys into the Paranormal
6 x 9 Softcover 120 pages
ISBN 978-1-88756-072-6

A powerful wizard, love-crossed ghosts, a mysterious dark warrior, and an enigmatic time traveler -- a mystical wordsmith entices you into the world of the paranormal with a collection of inspired stories. Each tale takes the journey of the dragonfly imbued with the momentum and energy of change, following a winding path that will ultimately lead you to find the truth buried beneath perception.

A Ghost of a Chance
6 x 9 Softcover 174 pages
ISBN 978-1-88756-050-4

Jack Brennan, an ambitious high-powered attorney, dies, only to find himself constrained to a peculiar afterlife as an earth-bound spirit trapped in an old

More Books by Evelyn Klebert

Virginia farmhouse with a very much living, reclusive writer of campy vampire novels. Hallie Barkly recovering from a painful and disillusioning divorce, has forged a career and exorcised her demons by writing under the pseudonym of Sebastian Winters. Their lives intersect, and two unconventional lovers are brought together under insurmountable circumstances. Together they must battle an unseen force hell-bent on possessing Hallie's life and bridge death itself to make possible what cannot be - to find a chance.

Breaking Through the Pale
6 x 9 Softcover 92 pages
ISBN 978-1-88756-045-0

Journey with metaphysical author Evelyn Klebert into a collection of short stories that travel beyond the pale into the unpredictable realm of the paranormal.
In "A Grey Mourning," a disillusioned man encounters a mysterious being on the foggy streets of New Orleans. "Contact" is a tale of automatic writing, when a young artist establishes communication with a spirit guide, and the victim of a car crash unravels the true nature of her existence in "Dancing on the Threshold." The final tale is called "Isolation," in which a confused and disoriented woman finds herself in an old, quaint house where she must piece together the mystical implications *surrounding her predicament.*

More Books by Evelyn Klebert

Explanations
6 x 9 Softcover 82 pages
ISBN 978-1-93493-515-6

In this, her second poetry collection, Evelyn Klebert takes us down the intricate path of a personal journey. Life, with its particular struggles, pitfalls, and ultimately triumphs, clearly begins to mirror a universal path, the quest for answers that we all ultimately pursue. In this reflective, esoteric collection, we can all explore and seek some of life's elemental mysteries and, hopefully, when all is said and done, emerge with some *Explanations*.

The Witches' Own
6 x 9 Softcover 124 pages
ISBN 978-1-61342-058-4

On the surface, things seem quiet and serene in the picturesque coastal village of Kilmarnock, Virginia. But something unseen roams its lush forests as the past and present collide, and the unthinkable begins to wreak its vengeance. Young Lucy Bonner is executed for witchcraft in the town's distant and brutal past. Her death triggers an unholy chain of events that grasp at the restless heart of novelist Peter McQuade, spurring him towards a quest to uncover the dark and terrifying truth.

More Books by Evelyn Klebert

The Left Palm
And Other Halloween Tales of the Supernatural
6 x 9 Softcover 104 pages
ISBN 978-1-93493-556-9

Halloween is the time of year when that veil between worlds is thinned, and you can just catch a quick glimpse into the realm of the unknowable. In this collection of short stories, Evelyn Klebert takes you to a place where ordinary life splinters into the sphere of the paranormal.

The journey begins with one woman's unstoppable quest for vengeance against a supernatural creature in "Wolves" and continues in an old historical graveyard where a horrifying discovery is uncovered in "Emma Fallon." In "The Soul Shredder," a psychiatrist's unusual patient opens his eyes to a disturbing new view of reality, while in "Wildflowers," a woman strikes up a supernatural friendship with impossible implications. And in "The Left Palm," a fortuneteller in the French Quarter receives a most unexpected and terrifying customer.

More Books by Evelyn Klebert

White Harbor Road
And Other Tales of Paranormal Romance
6 x 9 Softcover 130 pages
ISBN 978-1-61342-066-9

A psychic soul mate, a time traveler, a horror writer, and an enigmatic stranger take a selection of resilient, life-battered heroines to a place of paranormal healing and transformation. In this collection of short stories, White Harbor Road is the last stop where life's burdens and hardships evolve into something unexpected.

The Broken Vow
Vol. I of The Clandestine Exploits of a Werewolf
6 x 9 Softcover 140 pages
ISBN 978-1-61342-133-8

In the heart of every man, there is a history. In the heart of every monster, there is a story. In this first installment of *The Clandestine Exploits of a Werewolf,* Ethan Garraint is on a vendetta that begins in the heart of the Pyrenees with the fall of Montségur and leads him to the streets of New Orleans nearly five hundred years later. But the person he chases isn't really a man anymore, and Ethan has been a werewolf for almost a millennium. With the aid of a gifted seer, he is on a blood hunt that will culminate in a journey that crosses the line between heaven and earth and ends somewhere in between.

More Books by Evelyn Klebert

Travels into the Breach: Accounts of a Reclusive Mystic
6 x 9 Softcover 176 pages
ISBN 978-1-61342-323-3

At first glance, his life seems quiet, serene, and even uneventful. Malachi McKellan, a 65 five-year-old widower and author of esoteric books, lives largely as a recluse in a house situated just off the banks of Bayou St. John in New Orleans. But unbeknownst to most, he is also a bit of a detective, a specific kind of detective whose specialty is psychic attacks. Alongside his lifelong companion and spirit guide Simon Tull, a nineteenth century, twenty something English gent, Malachi battles the unseen, and is an unacknowledged hero to the most vulnerable - most of the population who have no idea what is really happening beneath the surface of the world in which they live.

In this collection of adventures, Malachi McKellan and Simon Tull wage war against the most insidious elements of the paranormal. In "The Three," Malachi and Simon come to the aid of a young woman being victimized by a group of dark witches. An old apartment building is the scene of an unimaginable battle against monstrous forces in "The Lost Soul." Malachi and Simon find themselves strategizing against a psychic vampire in "Obsession," and "The Hotel" turns back time to the 1980s where Malachi confronts a demonic spirit. In "Between," a past life is revisited as Malachi attempts to rescue a beloved sister from committing her existence to vengeance, and "The Wedding" takes a personal turn when Malachi must confront painful truths while endeavoring to protect his niece from a potentially devastating union. Travel into the Breach with a pair of paranormal warriors who choose to confront overwhelming forces on a battlefield unsuspected by most.

Considerations
6 x 9 Softcover 68 pages
ISBN 978-1-88756-062-7

Sometimes the struggle to understand the meaning and complexities of living comes down to a single moment of introspection or a fleeting yet meaningful reflection. This collection of poetry by Evelyn Klebert takes you down a winding path of self-discovery where the resolution may not always be absolute, but the journey is indeed unforgettable. It is a wide and varied map of inspired poetry for your examination and consideration.

Appointment with the Unknown: The Hotel Stories
6 x 9 Softcover 151 pages
ISBN 978-1613423608

A hotel, for most, represents a normal place, a predictable realm of commonality. One might even go as far to say a safe space, the reliable where nothing particularly unusual is expected to happen. Or is it? Dimensional traveling, spirit guides, mystical storms, and soul mates separated by time are only a few elements dotting this supernatural landscape. Drop into a collection of romantic paranormal stories where that place of commonality is only the threshold, the jumping-off point, for extraordinary adventures into the unknown.

More Books by Evelyn Klebert

The Tethering: A Portent of Crows
6 x 9 Softcover 201 pages
ISBN 978-1613425992

Deborah Brandt's beloved Aunt Gena always told her that she was special, a bit different, and would have to live her life, unlike other people. Of course, this she disregarded as the ramblings of her lovely but notably eccentric aunt. Although there were the things that Aunt Gena said that seemed true — like Deborah being sensitive to energy shifts, having potentially psychic impressions, and dreaming of a spirit guide — none of it could be real. But the most ridiculous thing that her Aunt Gena told her before she died was that someone special was out there for her. She said that he was an extraordinary man who was not only her perfect match but someone who she would learn from so that they could help the world in difficult times. How ridiculous! It sounds like a fairy tale, and no such person exists.

Daniel Wren is unique. He has been raised and trained from a young age to hone his psychic gifts. He lives in a world unimagined by most. And he has been waiting for years to contact his counterpart, soulmate, if you will. But the problem is that she is painfully unaware of the type of life that he lives and the life she would be entering into if they came together.

His dilemma becomes how best to proceed. How can he win her over and move forward before outside forces take that decision away from him?

More Books by Evelyn Klebert

The Lady in the Blue Dress
6 x 9 Softcover 214 pages
ISBN 978-1613426005

When she was a child, Mika Devalieur was introduced to her grandmother's most precious possession — a priceless and mysterious painting that she simply called The Lady in the Blue Dress. Upon Adele St. Clair's death, the painting is left in the care of her granddaughter with only one stipulation. Mika must hand over the family heirloom to a total stranger. Mika Devalieur desperately wants to deny her beloved grandmother's last request, but she can't. Torn between her Gran's last wishes and her desire to hold onto the Lady, she ultimately journeys to rural Virginia, where an enigmatic man shows her that this painting is only the beginning.

What quickly becomes clear is that James Clairmont knows much more about her and the Lady than he is letting on. He begins to slowly unravel a powerful supernatural connection that spans three generations of her family. Mika finds herself desperate to uncover the entire truth before she falls in love with a man filled with so many secrets — secrets about him, about her, and most especially about The Lady in the Blue Dress. (First published on Kindle Vella, episodes 1-23.)

Visit Evelyn's website at:
www.evelynklebert.com

Cornerstone Book Publishers
www.cornerstonepublishers.com

www.ingramcontent.com/pod-product-compliance
Lightning Source LLC
Chambersburg PA
CBHW020659260626
47157CB00008B/3093